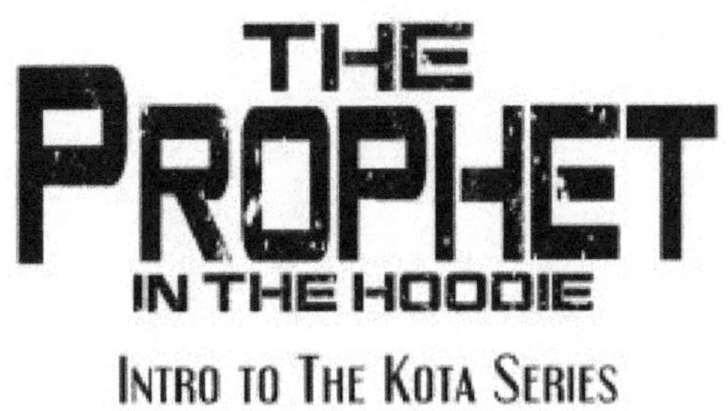

Intro to The Kota Series

Sunshine Somerville

This is a work of fiction. Similarities to real people, places, or events are entirely coincidental.

THE PROPHET IN THE HOODIE: INTRO TO THE KOTA SERIES

First edition. June 5, 2017.

ISBN: 979-8230338376

Written by Sunshine Somerville.

Table of Contents

Books by Sunshine Somerville

The Kota Series

The Prophet in the Hoodie: Intro to the Kota Series
The Kota
The Ebonite and Her Earthling
Pharmakon
Zenith Prophecies
The Woman of the Void
The Poet Heroic

The Alt-World Chronicles

The Eighth: Intro to The Alt-World Chronicles
Alterni
Malevolenci
Origini
The Fairy Master Capturi
Sirens and Assassi
Deus Endi

A Fairly Fairy Tale

See more at
SunshineSomerville.com

1

The Tattooist

"Where'd you get this design?" It seemed a casual question from the middle-aged tattoo artist, one he'd asked many times.

Hazen held his arm still, but the rest of him squirmed. "It's from a dream I had."

The needle lifted from his skin, and the tattooist raised a curious eyebrow. "A dream? That's it? And you're getting a tattoo of it?"

Hazen tried to chuckle and looked around the parlor at the handful of other workers and patrons. "That can't be the weirdest answer you've heard."

The tattooist shrugged in agreement and went back to work. Hazen toughed it out as the needle slid over and over the inside of his forearm. The '+' section complete, the artist got to work on the outer circle which would connect the points.

This was not Hazen's first tattoo. It wasn't his first from his dreams – well, *nightmares*, if he was being honest. But this Mark tattoo was the most important. He couldn't even explain why.

This Mark means something, he thought. I've envisioned it hundreds of times... On that little girl's shoulder when she's pulled across a burning camp. On that boy's as he fights soldiers. But those nightmares aren't at all like my normal visions. They're *far* in the future... Am I nuts? Well, no. I had my sanity confirmed a long time ago...

The tattooist's phone buzzed on the shelf behind his work station. He lifted the needle and looked at his phone, then made a face. "Sorry. It's my wife. Our kid's been home sick. Mind if I take this quick?"

"Go ahead."

The man turned away and answered his phone. "Hey, Rach. How's the kiddo?"

Hazen swallowed.

This, he thought, could be the last time he talks to his wife, if I'm wrong about *this* vision. If I screw this up... But I had to come. I have to try.

Hazen would never *not* try everything in his power ever again. Not after what happened with his brother.

But I wish there was a way to know, he thought. Some of my nightmares show things that are going to happen no matter what. Others show things that can be changed. It's maddening!

"I love you too. I'm just finishing up this last guy and then I'll hurry home. Bye." The tattooist hung up and returned his full focus to Hazen. "Sorry about that. Not super-professional, I know."

"No problem." Hazen smiled and tried not to look worried.

The needle buzzed again, followed by the piercing, scratching pain in Hazen's arm.

When the artist finished and wrapped Hazen's arm in plastic wrap like a leftover meal, Hazen pulled the sleeve of his hoodie back down. He paid at the parlor's front desk, leaving his tattooist a generous tip, and exited the shop. The door's bell jingled to announce his departure.

Hazen stepped out onto a cool, windy sidewalk. All the normal sounds of Toronto filled the air. He used his good arm to pull the hood of his sweatshirt over his buzzed hair, blocking the wind. Then he leaned against the side of the building, pretending to be busy on his phone. But he was starting to sweat, and his stomach tightened as he looked at the street and recognized it from his nightmare. It was almost time.

Soon, the door's bell jingled and his tattoo artist stepped onto the sidewalk. The man looked both ways along the street, pulled his collar over his ears, and looked down at his phone to check something. He stepped between two parked cars and looked both ways again before stepping out to cross the street.

Now, thought Hazen.

He darted after the man. Out of the corner of his eye, he saw the delivery truck rounding the corner. Just as the tattooist stepped into the truck's lane, Hazen caught up and grabbed the man's jacket. He heard the truck's brakes squeal, but he didn't look as he pushed the man forward and stumbled the last few steps to the far curb.

"What-" The man tripped over the curb but recovered. His eyes went from Hazen to the truck and back to Hazen.

The driver yelled, "Careful, buddy!" and drove on up the road.

Hazen, panting a bit, had to smile.

"Holy..." The tattooist looked around and ran a hand through his hair. "Thanks, man. I did *not* see that guy. I'm lucky you were here."

Hazen chuckled at this. "No worries. Have a nice day. Hope your kid gets better soon."

"Thanks." The man smiled, clapped Hazen's shoulder, and turned to walk up the sidewalk.

Hazen, incredibly relieved, let out a breath and turned to walk to his car. He looked at his watch, a college graduation gift from his father six years ago.

I still have half an hour, he thought. Should be enough time to reach the restaurant.

With a sigh, Hazen approached his parked Maserati Quattroporte. The beep to unlock the vehicle always sounded pretentious to Hazen, but damn it was a fun car to drive. The Maserati had been a competing graduation gift from his mother. Hazen had to admit she'd won that round.

When he sat behind the wheel, he pulled up his sleeve and examined the fresh tattoo. These always felt good. The pain helped glue him to this reality more than anything he'd tried. Certainly more than drugs – that'd been a whopper of a mistake. While in college, he'd experimented with anything that kept him awake, but certainly not for the purpose of pulling an all-nighter. He'd wanted to avoid sleep in order to avoid nightmares. The Dexedrine worked at first, but when he'd finally come down he'd slept deeper than ever. And his nightmares... Let's just say he didn't want any that vivid ever again. Nowadays, he was smarter about how to avoid the truly frightening visions, only sleeping four hours at a time. And he definitely avoided hallucinogenics. Hell, even Motrin activated nightmares about people infected with a disease that turned them into-

His phone rang. L.A. area code.

With a sigh, Hazen answered. "Hi, Mom."

"Hazen Randall Stephenson, please, tell me you're still going."

All three names, he thought. Yep, I'm in trouble.

"I'm on my way."

"Don't keep Maghen waiting. I told her mother you were excited to meet her, so at least try to smile, will you?"

"I'll be as charming as possible. I promise. Okay? Chill, Mackenzie Schultz-Stephenson-Whyte."

"Very funny. Call me when you're back at your hotel. Unless it's after ten. I have an early brunch with the girls."

His mother's demands were oddly selective.

"Okay. Bye."

He ended the call, then adjusted the mirror for a quick inspection. His blue eyes weren't too bloodshot. His skin was clean, though he hadn't shaved in a week. The circles under his eyes weren't too noticeable. He brushed a hand over his buzzed, blond hair, but there wasn't much to be done there.

Hazen started the Maserati, turned up the radio, and sped down the street.

How does Mom have friends in every city I visit? he thought. And I remember Mrs. Cannon – Maghen better not be anything like her mother.

2

The Blind Date

Maghen was exactly like her mother. Right down to the white tips at the ends of her nails, which she tapped on the table as they finished dessert. Dressed in a fashionable black dress, she'd expressed disapproval of his jeans and hoodie. It was true he might be a little underdressed for the restaurant, but she was certainly overdressed. Then again, Maghen didn't seem to mind standing out. Their table was in the middle of the long, busy, candlelit restaurant, and Hazen had lost track of how many men glanced Maghen's way.

She'd spent dinner talking about the boutique where she'd spent two grand before coming to dinner. Hazen had zoned out but tried to recover by mentioning a brand of shirts he liked. He'd apparently mispronounced the name, and Maghen's expression suggested she thought he was an idiot. That had led to their lengthy silence now.

"So," Hazen tried, "do you read much?"

She perked up. "Yeah, lots. I love Fantasy. Anything with magic, hunky heroes, love triangles, that kind of thing." She took a drink of her wine and tried to look smart. "But I'm so sick of clichés in books these days."

"Like what?"

"You know. Magicians, elves, loyal sidekicks, prophecies of the future."

Hazen flinched. He covered with a chuckle. "Think predicting the future's nonsense, huh?"

Maghen rolled her eyes. "It's so overdone."

He reached for his water. "It *is* annoying when you see them everywhere. But-"

"Right? If a book has a prophecy in it, I stop reading. Or, like if there's a quest or an evil lord or-"

With an exaggerated groan, a dark-skinned, young woman seated behind Maghen turned to face them. "Those aren't necessarily clichés! Those are just things *in* Fantasy stories! They're tropes. They only become clichés when they're *used* the same way they've been used hundreds of times. If a writer puts a twist on the trope, the magicians or prophecies or quests or whatever aren't clichés. If you see a trope and automatically stop reading, how will you know if things get more interesting? That's pretty shallow reading, Miss Chick-Lit Critic. It's all subjective, anyway. Some people love tropes that other people think are cliché – *you* said you like love triangles, which in my opinion-"

"Who asked you?" Maghen made a face at the woman. Then her gaze moved to a notebook beside the woman's wineglass. "Oh. You're a writer, aren't you? You all act like it's so hard." She made an exaggerated eye roll.

Hazen inspected the lone woman. She was his age, around thirty. Her dark hair was buzzed almost as short as his. Her eyes were beautiful. She wore retro gold earrings, which stood out because of her short hair. Her nose held a small gold stud. Her blue, satin shirt and black pants hugged her lean frame.

The woman inhaled to calm herself. "Sorry, but I couldn't sit by and listen anymore. First you order the most expensive thing on the menu – I saw you checking before your date got here. Who does that? Then you go on and on about shopping. Then you judge this poor guy for not being as shallow. And now you act like you're a literary expert. You're entitled to like what you like, but you were hurting my Creative Writing degree's heart when you got all uppity about it. And if you hate clichés so much, you could *try* to be less of a stereotypical rich girl."

"I don't have to listen to this!" Maghen looked around for the maitre d'. Then she caught Hazen trying not to laugh. "You think this harassment is funny?"

He held up his hands. "I didn't know you'd get so riled up."

"You're not going to defend me?"

"Well, you're being kind of mean. And you didn't seem to need assistance."

Maghen's phone went off where she'd left it face-up on the table. She looked at the screen and forgot everything else. "Oh, awesome! Kip is free!"

Hazen blinked. "Who?"

"My boyfriend." Maghen scooched her chair back and grabbed her purse under her seat.

"Your..." Hazen made a face.

Maghen stood and smoothed out her dress, then smiled at him like nothing was wrong with this development. "Thanks for dinner. I gotta go." And with that, she walked off through the restaurant toward the exit.

Hazen sighed and rested his head in his hands, elbows on the table. A glass being set on the table drew his attention back to the chair across from him. He looked up to see the Creative Writing defender taking Maghen's seat. She set her notebook and clutch purse on the table and smiled at him.

"Uh. Hi?"

She smiled. "Hi. Hazen, right?"

"Yeah. And you are?"

"Renny Nado. Nice to meet you." She reached across the table to shake his hand, then leaned back in her chair to inspect him.

He blinked at her. "Thanks for saving me from Maghen, but..."

"Sorry if I was bitchy to your date, but she *really* bugged me." Renny motioned behind her to where she'd been sitting. "I was minding my own business until I heard her talking on the phone before you got here. Kip sounds fascinating, by the way." She rolled her eyes, grinned, and took a drink from her wineglass. "Anyway..."

They entered a weird pause, and Hazen wondered if he should follow through on Maghen's attempt to flag down the maitre d'.

"There's no easy way into this, Hazen." Renny glanced at their nearby diners and lowered her voice. "Unlike Maghen, I don't think predicting the future is nonsense."

Any amusement Hazen felt over this situation was immediately gone. He swallowed. "I don't know what you're-"

"I had a dream about this restaurant. About sitting at that table, by myself, eavesdropping on your blind date."

He paused, unsure what to do with this. "Why should I believe you?"

"Because you see things too." She met his eyes, then smirked. "You're the man of my dreams, and I'm your better half."

He snorted a laugh, but he shook his head.

Okay, he thought, maybe she is crazy.

"When you have nightmares," she said with a point over her glass, "I have dreams. You foresee events that would happen if you didn't prevent them. I see the same events, but the alternative, better path you create. Or, if you like, I see the happy version that becomes reality after you change them from being nightmares."

Hazen took a breath. "Listen, I don't know who you are-"

"Like with the tattoo artist earlier today."

Hazen froze.

She lifted an eyebrow, seeing his reaction. "I dreamed of you saving him. Between these two dreams I've had of you in the same city, that's how I finally tracked you down." She made a disturbed face. "I'm guessing you saw the tattooist get smacked by the delivery truck?"

He paused again. "Yes."

Could this be real? he thought. I've never met anyone else who...

After a look around at the other diners, he leaned forward. "You had a dream about what I did with the tattoo artist? Do you mean you've seen other things I've changed?"

"Yeah. I've lost count how many. Your visions started when you were a teenager, right?"

He nodded.

"That's when mine started too. It was so weird to see you over and over again in my dreams, and I didn't know why it was happening. But then, one day back home in L.A., I saw a news story about cops who'd apprehended a teenage shoplifter. The cops took the boy back to the store right as two men tried to rob the place. I'd dreamed that exact thing, and I realized I was somehow dreaming of *real* things that happened in the future."

Hazen smiled. "I remember that one. The cops didn't exactly believe I'd known the robbers were coming, but they didn't know what else to do with me, so they let me go. 'Bigger fish to fry,' they said."

Renny returned his smile. "After that, I started looking up news stories about my dreams. Of course, you never stuck around to take credit for your heroics, so I never actually learned your name. But with every dream and every news story, you'd done exactly what I'd seen. I saw you tell the police in time to stop the terrorist attack in Chicago. I saw you beg a family to leave their house before the flood swept it away in New Orleans. You reported the fire before it happened in Tokyo."

He grinned in memory.

She hesitated. "But since I always envision the happy endings of things, I never worried about any of this. It was cool to track your heroics, but I never thought you needed my help for anything. I assumed your visions were like mine, and I thought you knew what to do because you saw yourself doing it."

Hazen nodded. It made sense. He couldn't blame her.

"Eventually a few news stories did get your name. Then I set up alerts on my computer to collect any story mentioning Hazen Stephenson." She looked at him with sympathy. "That's when I heard the news story about your brother. I'm sorry to bring it up."

Oh, God, he thought.

He almost couldn't get out his question. "What did you see? Could I have stopped-"

"No." Her eyes widened, and she shook her head, causing her earrings to jingle. "No, I'm sorry. I didn't mean I saw anything. It's just... When I heard about your brother's accident, I felt bad for you and wanted to see if you were okay. That's when I learned your mom checked you into the hospital for psychiatric treatment. And *that's* when I realized maybe your visions weren't always as happy as mine."

Hazen took a drink of water to steady himself.

I can finally talk about this, he thought. She won't think I'm crazy.

"When I was seventeen, I had a nightmare where I saw Chuck die in a car accident. I tried everything to stop it. I begged him not to go out that night. I hid his keys. He told me he'd stay home. But I woke up the next morning and heard my mom screaming and crying. I knew immediately I hadn't stopped the nightmare from coming true. I was so traumatized I told my mom about it... Big mistake."

Renny gave him a second.

He took a breath. "So, yeah. I have nightmares and try to stop them. But I can't stop all of them. The problem is, I never know which can be changed and which can't." He rubbed his sweaty hands on his jeans. "Do you think what happened to my brother was for sure a nightmare I couldn't have changed?"

It was a sick thing to hope was true, but...

Renny nodded, her expression again conveying sympathy. "Like I said, I only see events you can turn into happy endings. For years, I never knew you had different dreams from mine, *more* dreams than mine. I've never seen anything you couldn't prevent. I didn't see your brother's accident at all. I don't think it was something you were allowed to change."

Hazen sighed. He looked down at the crumbs on his dessert plate and tried to collect himself.

Renny opened her clutch, took out a few bills, and tossed them on her original table. "Come on. Let's get some air."

Hazen had already paid, so he stood from the table as Renny gathered her things. Together, they exited the restaurant and stepped onto the dark sidewalk along the lakefront.

It was windy but not too cold, and the streetlights along the cement path shone the way into the city. Renny was as tall as he was, and they walked in step along the sidewalk.

"So," he asked, "you don't see my nightmares?"

"No. Never."

He tried to make sense of this. "If you don't see a correlating dream, my nightmares are what will happen. But if you see a dream, *that's* what will happen."

"I think so, yeah. That's why I finally realized I should find you. I can tell you which visions you can do something about." Renny looked over at him as they went by a streetlight. "When you can't change something, it's not your fault. For whatever reason, I guess some of your nightmares are meant to happen."

Hazen took a second with this unexpected, life-changing relief.

For years, he thought, I've wrestled with the guilt. The responsibility. Not knowing if I wasn't doing enough... Now I have a partner. I'm not alone.

He exhaled a long breath into the dark night. With another thought, he looked at Renny. "Do you get other visions without me in them?"

"Yeah, though not as often. Those dreams..." She whistled. "They're not from any *near* future."

Again, relief washed over him. "They're weird, right? Snippets that don't make sense. And they're *far* in the future. It's cool to see things like hover cars, palm scanners, new glowing money. But things are wrong too. I see pollution, decay, whole cities in ruins. I keep seeing people's faces, and they all look scared. And there's this horrible virus that turns the infected into..." He studied her face. "Is that like your dreams?"

"Somewhat, but I don't see anything scary." She scrunched her face in thought. "It must be like how you have nightmares and I have dreams. You see the bad stuff; I see happier things. I mean, from what I can tell, the future *itself* isn't great, but I always feel a sense of hope, love, loyalty. I can't explain it very well. Nothing's ever decipherable. My dreams of the distant future are way more jumbled than my normal dreams. I see faces, buildings..."

He nodded. "And sometimes there's this swirling red and yellow light."

"Yes! And this..." Renny pulled back her sleeve.

Hazen was only slightly surprised she'd tattooed the Mark on her arm. He pulled up the sleeve of his hoodie to show her his fresh, wrapped Mark.

Renny smiled. "You see the kids too?"

"Yeah. Four of them. Mostly when they're really little. But also some when they're grown up. They seem...important."

And, thought Hazen, like they might be the whole reason I – we – have these visions.

He scowled. "Do you have any idea why this happens to us?"

"Nope, but I might know people who do. In college, I went on a mission trip to Africa with a group called the Kota. Three of the Kota mentors were particularly kind to me, and we've stayed in touch. I told them about my dreams, and they've helped me a lot. They actually paid for my trip here because they thought it was important I find you." She looked like she expected him to freak out. "Sorry to spring this on you, but they want me to bring you to them. They won't tell me anything specific, but I have a feeling this is important, Hazen. They say we're not the only ones with visions."

"There are others? Do the Kota have visions themselves?"

Renny shook her head. "I don't think so. At least, my mentors don't. But they've been looking into this for a while. And I think they can give us answers, maybe help us with whatever future we're being shown." She looked at him as they crossed a street. "I feel like something big is coming. Do you?"

"Yeah. I mean, I've been doing what I can with my nightmares for years, but there's always *something* more with those stranger visions of the future. I just don't have all the pieces."

She nodded and bit her lip in thought. "I know it's asking a lot, Hazen, but would you come with me to meet the Kota? If this is as important as we think... Let's hope the Kota can help."

He let out a breath as he spotted his parked car. "So where are the Kota? Where do we go next?"

Renny laughed. "Vegas."

"Okay... Why's that funny?"

"You'll understand when you meet them."

He didn't get this, but he motioned to his car. "This is me. Can I give you a ride somewhere?"

"Yes, please. I walked from my hotel." She looked relieved he accepted all this.

But why shouldn't I? he thought. This is so weird, but I trust her. She might turn out to be the best friend I've ever had. We're like each other's yin and yang, or something. I'm not alone anymore. And if these Kota people have even more answers, you bet your butt I'm going to meet them.

As they climbed in the car, Renny smiled at him. "So, Hazen, what kind of books do *you* read?"

3

The Trapezist

People scream and run across the sidewalk in front of the hotel. Flashing and twinkling casino signs illuminate the night. A man with a gun turns and flees the scene. A cop car approaches, its sirens and lights further adding to the chaos.

Hazen runs to a woman lying on the ground. He kneels beside her. She's covered in blood from a gunshot to her chest.

The cop car pulls up.

"That way!" Hazen shouts as he points up the sidewalk. "The shooter went that way!"

One cop sprints off down the sidewalk, and his partner returns to the car to radio for backup.

The woman grabs Hazen's shirtsleeve. "Win..." She gasps for breath, but a second later her head drops and she's still.

An ambulance arrives, but Hazen knows it's too late.

"I'm so sorry," he says to the dead woman. "I'm so, so sorry."

Hazen woke and looked around to place himself. He was on the bed of his hotel room. He'd only meant to rest his eyes, but he'd fallen asleep.

Oh, no, he thought. Does this nightmare happen tonight? Tomorrow night? Shit...

He stood from the bed, winced from pain in his arm, and grabbed the tube of cream off his nightstand. While he rubbed cream into his healing Mark tattoo, he walked to his window.

It was still bright afternoon. He'd been to Vegas during his 'misspent youth' period, his floundering college years. As he looked out his high hotel window now, he saw everything along the strip looked much the same as he remembered. A few old casinos had been demolished and replaced by newer, grander buildings. But the general ambiance was the same.

Should I tell Renny my nightmare? he thought.

While flying to Vegas on his private jet, Hazen and Renny had discussed every vision they could remember. Many of Hazen's nightmares had correlated with Renny's dreams. But there were also events only Hazen had envisioned, and Renny had never known these things Hazen *hadn't* been able to change. Also, Renny sometimes had dreams of Hazen that he didn't envision at all – such as his blind date with Maghen. If she ever had another dream about him, she promised to tell him.

After tossing his tube of cream back on the nightstand, Hazen walked to the door connecting their adjoining rooms. He knocked. A second later, Renny opened the door. She wore the same jeans and T-shirt she'd traveled in. Since she hadn't yet changed for the show they were going to, Hazen guessed he hadn't napped that long.

Renny saw his face and furrowed her brow. "What's wrong?"

"I had a nightmare."

Why now? he thought. Can't I have one day to tend to my own life?

Renny stepped into his room and sat in a chair facing his bed. Hazen took the hint and sat on the bed, facing her. Then he told her every detail he could remember of the nightmare.

He took a shaky breath before he dared ask, "Did you dream?"

With a sad look, Renny shook her head. "No, I'm sorry. I took a nap too, but...nothing."

"Great." He frowned. "So this nightmare's going to happen no matter what."

"Did you know the woman?"

"Never seen her. And you're the only person I know in Vegas right now. But..."

Renny made a face. "But maybe it's one of the other vision-seers we're here to meet. Lhamo said one is a woman."

Lhamo, Seth, and Mino were her three Kota mentors. She'd called them from the Canadian airport to say she and Hazen were on their way to Vegas. Once they landed, the mysterious Lhamo had called with instructions, and in a few hours they were supposed to meet up after a show.

Hazen let out a breath. "The woman could be whoever we're meeting today. But I don't know."

Renny looked at the television's display module showing the time. "We'd better get ready. Are you going to be okay?"

Pulling himself together, Hazen nodded. He tried a smile. "It's not my first awful nightmare. Won't be my last. I'll try to put it out of mind until it starts to happen in the present."

Renny nodded and, still looking concerned, returned to her room and shut the door.

I have to focus on why we're here, thought Hazen. I *can* forget that nightmare for a while – I'm not new to this. And in a weird way, it's a relief to know Renny didn't dream an alternative future. That means there's nothing I can do to save this woman, whoever she is. The best I can do is help her die in peace when the time comes. And I send the cops after the shooter. That's something.

Hazen walked to his unpacked clothes and laid out the best suit he'd brought this trip. If he wanted help from these Kota people, he figured it'd be best to make a good impression. After a quick shower, he dressed and fixed his tie before putting on his vest. It was definitely too hot for the suit jacket.

Could these Kota people really know what's going on with our visions? he thought. I looked them up on our flight here. They sound pretty docile – charity events, global outreach, refugee work. They sound respectable. So how do they know anything about trippy visions of the future?

Fully dressed, Hazen examined himself in the mirror and figured he looked presentable. With a shrug at his reflection, he walked to the connecting door and knocked again.

"Come in. I'm almost ready."

Hazen opened the door and entered Renny's room, which matched his. As he looked toward the open bathroom door, Renny hopped out on one foot, trying to put on a sandal. She wore a bright red, sleeveless summer dress, showing off her beautiful dark skin. The dress hung to her knees, and she wore sandals which exposed a toe ring. Her short hair looked wet from a shower, but she'd put on eye makeup and matching red lipstick.

Hazen looked down at himself. "Am I overdressed?"

She smirked. "A little. And it's hot out, so you're going to bake."

"Hmm." He took off his vest and tie, tossing them over a nearby chair. Next undoing the top button of his white dress shirt, he asked, "Better?"

"Much. But you still look tired. Did you get any sleep before your nightmare?"

"A little." He blinked. His eyes were dry.

"You need sleep, Hazen."

"Yeah, well..."

Easy for her to say, he thought. Renny only sees the happily ever after dreams, not my nightmares.

Renny went to a table and picked up her clutch and phone, then noticed something on the screen. "Lhamo says..." She started laughing.

"What?"

She held out the screen to him. "The names. Look at their names."

The text said, "Jazzmon and Oryan will meet you in your seats at 2:00 p.m. Enjoy the show!"

Hazen smiled, having learned earlier that Renny found odd modern names hilarious. "More importantly, look at the time."

Renny looked at her phone again. "Crap. We'd better scoot."

THE PROPHET IN THE HOODIE: INTRO TO THE KOTA SERIES

They exited the hotel room and walked along the hall's lush carpet to the elevator. After stepping inside, Renny tapped the lit control screen for the lobby, and they leaned against the back wall as the lift descended.

Hazen was getting excited. "So this Jazzmon and Oryan. They're vision-seers like us?"

"Guess so. That's what Lhamo told me earlier."

She doesn't know much more than I do, thought Hazen.

The elevator doors opened. They stepped into the hotel lobby, where other guests strolled toward the hall of shops or else headed for the revolving door that led outside to the sunny sidewalk.

Hazen swallowed as he looked out at the sidewalk.

My nightmare was at night, he thought. I have hours and hours before it comes true. There's plenty to focus on until then.

He followed Renny across the lobby to the casino wing of the building. A darker ambiance and the recognizable dinging noises of slot machines greeted them.

I forgot how annoying that sound is, he thought. Then again, last time I was here I was stoned out of my gourd. It's a wonder I remember this place at all.

He shook his head at his youthful foolishness and followed Renny through the casino to the back section. Here stood golden, ornate, glass doors. A small group of people stood in lines here, and a pair of casino workers scanned tickets before allowing people to step through the doors. Renny got their tickets out of her clutch and let one of the workers scan them.

"Enjoy the show," said the man with a permanently pasted grin.

"Thank you." Renny pushed open the door to lead Hazen out.

Outside, Hazen looked around a tiled courtyard. This casino was fairly new, and the white tiles sparkled without scratches or scuff marks. Stands selling trinkets and snacks dotted the open area, and exotic music played over speakers hidden in potted plants. Desert sun shone on the scene, but tall pillars supported giant woven fans that cast shade on those below. The afternoon air was dry and warm. Hazen noticed he was still overdressed as he inspected the crowd.

Renny pointed to the far side of the courtyard. "Let's go find our seats."

They walked over to where the courtyard ended and steps descended into a wide, C-shaped amphitheater. Different rows of seats were marked with Roman numerals, as if this added a touch of class and intrigue to the casino's theme. The seats around the amphitheater were padded like good seats at a ballgame, and hundreds of people were already waiting for the show to start. The stage itself was wide and held a pool in its center. The back wall of the stage rose at least three stories before a ceiling jutted out over the stage. On this floating ceiling's underside, different colored lights, metal walkways, and wiring were placed strategically. In the background of all this, a wing of the casino itself rose tall into the blue sky.

Renny whistled. "Nice."

Hazen agreed and followed her down the amphitheater stairs. They looked at their tickets a few times to make sure they were in the right section, and eventually they found their row and shuffled past tourists already seated. When they at last reached their two open spaces, Hazen folded down his seat, sat, and activated the chair's cooling unit.

Oh, that feels amazing, he thought.

Then he noticed the man and woman seated beside him. The tall, lanky, blond man wore dress shorts and a button-down T-shirt. He had a program for the show on his lap. His retro glasses made him look like a geek, but a sports watch also caught Hazen's eye. The woman was pretty, athletic, with long blond hair and blue eyes. She wore white shorts and a flowing top with abstract flowers, but she didn't strike Hazen as girly. In fact, she looked quite stoic. Both the man and woman were in their early thirties. Both looked at Hazen and Renny with equal curiosity.

Renny had noticed this too and leaned over Hazen to see them. "Hi, are you Jazzmon and Oryan? I'm Renny."

The man extended a hand to Renny. He spoke with a Norwegian accent. "It's *Or-i-on* – pronounced like the constellation, actually. My mom loved all the space discoveries when she was pregnant with me." He chuckled good-naturedly and held out a hand to shake with Hazen. "Hazen, correct?"

"Yes. Hi." He smiled and shook the man's hand. "My dad works for the World Space Program, so I totally get it."

"Ah!" Oryan's eyes lit up behind his glasses.

Jazzmon waved from her seat with a small smile. "It's nice to meet you both."

Thank God, thought Hazen. She's not the woman in my nightmare.

He tried to sort out her accent. "Danish?"

"Yes. I'm from Copenhagen."

Renny still leaned over him. "So how do you guys know Lhamo?"

Yes, thought Hazen. Time for answers.

Oryan looked at Jazzmon in confusion before facing them again. "We don't know Lhamo. Sonyeah's the one who told us to come."

"Sonyeah?" Now Renny looked confused. "I don't know who that is."

"She's from our Kota community back home. Now she lives here to be near the community in Utah where she trains. Sonyeah's-"

A burst of music over the speaker system made them jump and look to the stage. A spotlight from the stage ceiling kicked on and changed colors as the light spread into abstract shapes over the pool. Music swept like a breeze over the amphitheater, and people either hushed or cheered as the show began.

Oryan leaned to say in Hazen's ear, "Guess we'll talk later."

Hazen made a face of agreement and politely clapped with the crowd.

A body rose out of the water where the spotlight swirled. The muscular man wore a skintight costume the color of the water, and he tilted his head at odd angles. Wherever he looked around the stage, other costumed gymnasts and dancers appeared. Three women spun down from the ceiling's underbelly on bright yellow drapes, and the crowd gasped in admiration. One man suddenly dropped from the ceiling in a dive, splashing into the pool below. Then another mirrored the dive from the other side. Back on the stage, three nymph-looking women pulled out a tall, wide prop designed to look like trees. Different parts lit up in different hues of green as their fake leaves appeared to blow in a nonexistent wind. More gymnasts appeared. More dancers. A pair of fire-throwers rose from the floor as the music intensified.

Hazen found himself transfixed like everyone else as he watched the show.

A trapezist made a daring flip.

Oryan leaned over. "That's Sonyeah."

"Who is? The trapezist?"

"Yep."

Hazen looked at him, but Oryan just raised his eyebrows above his glasses and clapped with the crowd.

Not for the first time, this all seemed utterly surreal.

When the show ended, everyone rose to leave. Hazen assumed they'd climb back up the steps, but Jazzmon led them in the opposite direction, down the stairs. Oryan seemed to think this was right, so Hazen shrugged at Renny and followed them as they went against the flow of show-goers.

When they reached the bottom level, Jazzmon continued to the far part of the amphitheater that butted up against the main casino building. The Dane led them to a door labeled 'Authorized Personnel Only,' pulled out a keycard from her shorts' pocket, and swiped the panel above the doorhandle. A light on the panel clicked green, and

Jazzmon opened the door. Oryan entered behind her, Renny gave Hazen a shrug and followed, and with a deep breath Hazen went after her.

With the door closed behind him, Hazen blinked to adjust to the dark, cement hallway. The sublevel of the casino was without glitz, and he followed the others through a windowless hall, past several doors leading into tech rooms. Soon enough they turned left into a well-lit hall. Gymnasts and other performers walked from room to room, chatting and laughing as they entered different dressing rooms. Hazen's group walked past a wide doorway showing a props room, where the crew was already busy preparing for the next show. Finally, Jazzmon knocked at a door, waited for permission to enter, and led them into a small dressing room.

Hazen entered to see a lit makeup table and chair, a side sofa with piles of clothes tossed across the back, a side bathroom, and a wide closet of costumes.

Sonyeah, the trapezist Oryan had pointed out, sat at the makeup table. She was unwrapping a brace from her ankle. The bottom leg of her leotard was pulled up to reveal a muscular calf. Wrinkles through her face paint suggested she was older than Hazen would've guessed, but she was obviously fit. Still in full costume, she wore long, white eyelashes and a green wig curled and sparkling with jewels.

Three men also stood in the cramped room, and their appearance actually struck Hazen as more odd. Each wore black robes of the Buddhist style from shoulders to ankles. Their arms were bare, and their exposed feet wore slip-on shoes. They were in their sixties, Hazen guessed, with heads and faces completely shaved. One of the men was tall with arms still muscular for his age, and aside from his attire he looked like an average, American, working class grandfather-type. The monk in the middle was shorter, his eyes and skin color suggesting Chinese lineage. The third man was also Asian but far pudgier, and his face looked kind as he smiled at the newcomers.

Monks? thought Hazen. Really? In Vegas...

Beside him, Renny grinned at his obvious surprise. Then she stepped forward to hug each man in warm greeting. "Seth, hi! Lhamo! Mino, you've lost weight!"

Jazzmon and Oryan said quick greetings to Sonyeah, who looked relieved to see them but focused on taking off bits of her costume.

Hazen just stood there.

Lhamo, the middle monk, smiled at him and said in perfect English, "Greetings from Heaven, Hazen." He bowed.

Hazen returned the bow, hoping he was doing it right. He stood erect again and said uncertainly, "Hello."

"I'm Seth." The tall American's voice was deep and sounded Southern. With a crooked grin wrinkling the side of his face, he motioned to their third companion. "This is Mino. He's taken a vow of silence and so won't be explaining much."

The pudgy Mino smiled with a bow.

Lhamo faced the newcomers. "I assume you'd all like answers. And fast?"

Oryan looked respectful, his hands folded in front of him. "Yes, please."

Lhamo nodded. "First, I hope you can keep what we're about to say to yourselves. From what we know of your lives thus far, I'm sure you realize most people wouldn't understand or accept what we're about to discuss."

Hazen nodded, and he saw the others doing the same. He shuffled on his feet.

Please, have answers, he thought with a healthy level of desperation.

Lhamo nodded again. "I'd first like to clarify anything you might've heard about the Kota. We're not a cult, for starters." He sighed. "That's a popular assumption. Our people *do* try to keep to the tenants of our ancient faith. We've given ourselves the new label of 'Kota' to distinguish ourselves from the many denominations we feel have lost focus. The whole point behind the Kota is that we try to show the love of Heaven to mankind in any way we can."

Hazen glanced at Renny, remembering her Kota mission trip to Africa.

Seth jumped in. "We of course approach everything with our spiritual beliefs at the base of our understanding. That's caused many to think our interpretations of current events make us crazy fanatics."

"Yeah..." Hazen had read a few articles on the Kota during their flight to Vegas. "People say you think we've entered the end times."

Seth rolled his eyes. "Global pollution, famine, earthquakes, religious persecution, hedonism, wars... Okay, all the signs are there, but they've been around for centuries. How people interpret the biblical prophecies has led to confusion and turmoil-"

"They don't need a religious history lesson." Sonyeah, her wig now off to expose twisted, pinned up blond locks, stood from her seat. She walked to the sofa, grabbed a handful of clothes, and turned to the side bathroom. "Tell them why we need them, Seth." She pulled the door closed for privacy.

Hazen heard the sound of water running and assumed she was washing off her face paint.

Seth got back on track. "We don't think we're dealing with *the* end times. But clearly you vision-seers are seeing what you see for a reason, and we Kota are trying to figure out that reason. Because we don't want the world to think we're nuts, we've tried to keep all this as much under wraps as possible until we know what we're dealing with."

Lhamo nodded. "Years ago, when Sonyeah first proved to us her dreams were real, we realized something significant was happening. After much study, we've reached the conclusion that vision-seers are shown the future much like the ancient prophets must've been shown the future. They recorded what they understood from their visions, although what they saw probably didn't make sense to them. The distant-future visions *you* see probably don't make sense to you, either.

But we believe your visions are as important as the ancient prophets'. We believe we need to work with you to record them."

Seth nodded. "And that means you four must work together so we can collect a complete picture of the future."

Hazen took a breath.

This does make sense, he thought. After all the things I've seen, I don't have reason to doubt any of this. I've had the sense all along that those stranger visions of the future are important. If we're like prophets...

"What's interesting," said Lhamo, "is that you've each only received glimpses of this future, nothing you can interpret like with your normal visions. Even Sonyeah and her vision partner never understood their fragments." He raised an eyebrow at Hazen. "And *you've* trained yourself to avoid visions of the future. I understand, since they must be disturbing. It's admirable you've focused on saving people from the more immediate nightmares you've seen." He smiled. "But, it's important you accept the distant-future visions now and change focus."

Jazzman had her arms crossed in thought. "Sonyeah told us her normal dreams stopped once you trained her to focus on the distant-future visions. Are you saying you want to do that with us?"

This was the first Hazen had heard this, and he exchanged a look with Renny.

Lhamo tried to explain. "There's a pattern to how your visions work. Jazzmon and Hazen see nightmares of what will inevitably happen, but they also see what can be avoided. Meanwhile, Renny and Oryan see what *will* happen only when Jazzmon or Hazen can change the outcome. And, Renny and Oryan dream of Jazzmon and Hazen because – we think – it's their responsibility to take care of their more troubled vision partners."

Hazen's group exchanged nods like this made sense.

"We think," Lhamo continued, "that with *all* of you together, you can now help each other make sense of the distant-future visions. From what we've learned of them so far, we think they might be more important than continuing your work of saving everyday people. That sounds harsh, I know, but there's a bigger picture to consider."

Jazzmon frowned. "Well, nothing in my normal nightmares has ever been as bad as what I've seen in the distant-future nightmares. You might be right that they're more important."

Hazen thought on this.

Yeah, he thought. It's a tough call, though...

"So," Hazen asked, "if we join you Kota and let you train us to access the distant-future visions, we'll stop getting our normal visions? You're sure."

Lhamo glanced at the closed bathroom door. "Yes, we're pretty sure. Sonyeah and Vin, her vision partner, were the first pair we worked with – the *only* other vision partners we'd discovered until you four. Vin saw nightmares like Hazen and Jazzmon. Sonyeah had dreams like Renny and Oryan. When we started training them to focus on their distant-future visions, Sonyeah's normal dreams stopped pretty quickly. Vin..." Lhamo looked at Seth. "Well, Vin said his usual nightmares continued. Since Sonyeah could no longer tell him if his nightmares were alterable, Vin would go off for days at a time to check...or so he said."

"What does that mean?" asked Oryan.

Seth shook his head with an angry scowl. "Vin lied. He wasn't checking on his nightmares. He was going off to kill people himself."

"Oh!" Renny put a hand to her mouth.

Lhamo nodded at this reaction. "The man snapped. He questioned everything we taught him. I think whatever he saw in the distant future was too much for him. And maybe he really did keep seeing unavoidable, terrible nightmares. Seeing such darkness might've been too much for him."

Hazen met eyes with Jazzmon.

Great, thought Hazen. Will *we* turn into psychopaths because we've seen too much?

Lhamo's frown deepened. "Whatever he sees, Vin chose to create darkness of his own. And he doesn't want us to stop him."

Renny was scowling. "Where's Vin now?"

"No idea." Seth frowned and, like Lhamo, glanced at the closed bathroom door. "Sonyeah hasn't dreamed of him since he left our Utah community over a year ago. That might be partly our fault, since we trained her to focus on her distant-future visions. Those visions might've overridden Sonyeah's ability to detect Vin's alterable nightmares. We don't really know."

Lhamo shook his head. "This is uncharted territory in the modern era. And we weren't prepared for Vin to become...what he became."

They were silent a moment, and Hazen realized the water in the bathroom had stopped.

I wonder how much Sonyeah heard, he thought. Poor woman. I already feel so connected to Renny. I can't imagine someone you share so much with turning into a monster. It must be awful to feel that alone all over again.

Lhamo folded his hands in front of his robes. "In any case, now we need you four to pick up where they left off. Sonyeah still has dreams, but they're only pieces. Without Vin, it's hard for her to confirm what she's seeing. And since we don't know how much Vin was lying, we don't know if we can trust anything he recorded."

Seth nodded. "We have to start over. If this is as important for the future as we suspect, we have to be right. And that means working with you four to piece this future together. Who knows what this could mean? Saving the world, maybe."

Oryan pushed a hand through his hair. "I need a drink." Then he remembered he was talking to monks. "Oh, sorry. I..."

Seth grinned. "I could use a tall beer myself."

Lhamo smiled and turned to the closed bathroom door. "Sonyeah, we're going to head up to the casino. Come join us when you're ready, okay?"

"Sure," came the sullen answer.

Lhamo exchanged a look with Seth, and Hazen guessed they were concerned about the woman.

These are good men, thought Hazen. Monks... I never imagined I'd sign up with monks.

Following Lhamo, everyone stepped into the hall.

Renny walked beside Hazen and smiled. "Here we go, huh?"

He nodded. "Here we go."

Hazen lost track of time as he sat with his new friends around a high-top table in the casino's bar. The unending sounds of gambling were giving him a headache, but he enjoyed these people's company. As Jazzmon and Renny talked about...whatever, the silent Mino spotted a group of frat boys and pointed them out to his fellow monks. The frat guys were pointing at the drinking monks and laughing in surprise. Mino waved with a big smile. The guys waved back and gave thumbs up before moving on.

"Monks in a bar!" One frat guy laughed to his friends. "Vegas has everything, man!"

Oryan took another swig of his beer. "I can't believe this either. I'm drinking in a bar in Vegas..."

"With monks," finished Hazen with a drunken lisp.

Seth grinned. "With monks who are purposefully getting you drunk." The tall monk leaned his elbows on the high-top table, looking oddly casual considering his attire.

"Purposefully..." Hazen set down the martini Lhamo had insisted he drink. He'd tried to argue that he didn't drink because inebriation triggered nightmares of the distant future, but now he understood. "You're trying to get me drunk so I envision the future?"

He'd said this a little loud considering the crowds. Then again, this was Vegas.

Seth took another drink. "Well, we need to kick-start this, Hazen. Your mind in particular needs to reopen to the deeper visions. You've been skimming along the surface of what you can see for years – not that your work hasn't been admirable. But this is bigger than saving an occasional tattoo artist."

Hazen turned to Renny, who was suddenly very interested in the ceiling. "Have you told them *everything* about me?"

Renny grinned at him, took another drink of her rum and Coke, and resumed talking with Jazzmon. "If each of us sees slightly different things in this future, how can we be sure of the message behind what we're being told? I mean, if we're going to write these visions as prophecies, how do we make them accurate?"

"Well," said Jazzmon, "There've been prophecies before. I mean, Judaism, Christianity, Islam – they all have recorded prophecies. Can't we do whatever they did before and...I don't know."

Oryan was good at being in a few conversations at once, even halfway squiffed. He turned to the women. "What, like a scientific method for how to decipher visions? I don't think there's an exact science to this. The ancient prophets were mystics. It's not like there are records detailing their process."

Hazen looked at Lhamo. "But we're going to write our visions exactly like we see them?"

Lhamo paused in thought. "We're not sure what would be best, honestly. With Sonyeah and Vin, they only got as far as recording what they saw and trying to sort out the puzzle pieces. That's when we realized Vin was lying."

"But as for how to best *write* the prophecies..." Seth smiled at Renny. "That might be an area where your gifts will be useful."

Her eyes widened. "No pressure."

Lhamo smiled at her. "Once you four piece together your visions of the future, we'll leave it to you to decide the best way to write the prophecies – *you*, after all, are the prophets. We Kota are only here to facilitate you in any way we can, and we don't want to interfere. But the wording of the prophecies will be especially important since we'll need to translate them into the language used at our temple."

Renny looked nervous. "So much could get lost in translation..."

"Yes," said Lhamo, "but we don't know how far in the future these prophecies will be needed. We must preserve the prophecies during the years to come, and that means intrusting them to the monks in our temple."

Oryan took a swig. "Why not just publicize the prophecies as soon as we're done with them?"

"Because people would think we're nuts." Hazen frowned into his glass.

Lhamo nodded at his words.

Mino tapped him on the shoulder and pointed.

Lhamo looked back through the casino and waved. "Ah, there's Sonyeah."

Hazen turned. It took him a second to spot Sonyeah, considering she was no longer dressed like a trapezist or wearing face paint. Sonyeah held up a hand to wave at them, but she was on her phone and looked distracted. As she ended her call and lowered her phone, she frowned and seemed to debate a second before turning and heading back toward the lobby.

Hazen's blood drained from his face. He recognized her now.

Oh, my God, he thought. It's Sonyeah. She's the woman from my nightmare!

This sobered him considerably. Without thinking, he shoved back his chair and dashed across the casino after her.

"Hazen?" called Renny.

He tried not to throw up as he hurried past tourists and gamblers and jingling coins. Once in the lobby, he had a clearer path to the hotel's revolving doors. He saw Sonyeah exiting onto the sidewalk, and the streetlights illuminated her face as she looked left, then right. Hazen reached the doors behind a family slowly exiting, and he tried not to panic as he shuffled forward.

Sonyeah, outside, looked into a crowd approaching the hotel doors. Her eyes widened as she apparently recognized someone, and her mouth opened to scream.

The gunshot that went off blasted above every other sound. Sonyeah fell backward to the ground, blood soaking her shirt.

People screamed and ran from the scene. The glare of the lights sparkled against the door's glass as Hazen finally pushed through. He looked in time to see a man put a gun in his coat. Hazen couldn't see his face, and the man hurried away through the panicked crowd. A cop car's loud siren added to the confusion, but Hazen regathered himself and ran to Sonyeah, kneeling beside her.

When the cop car pulled up, Hazen stayed with Sonyeah but shouted, "That way!" He pointed up the sidewalk. "The shooter went that way!"

One cop sprinted off down the sidewalk, and his partner went to radio for backup.

Sonyeah grabbed Hazen's shirtsleeve. "Vin..."

Oh, shit! thought Hazen. In my nightmare she was saying, 'Vin' not 'Win.' How'd I miss this?

She gasped for breath, but a second later her head dropped and she was still.

An ambulance pulled up behind the cop car.

Hazen saw blood on his shirt where Sonyeah had touched him, but he didn't care. He sat back on the sidewalk and started to cry. "I'm so sorry. I'm so, so sorry."

4

The Infected

Swirling, fire-colored light. Inside a dark, metallic container, dozens of bodies float in zero gravity. The smell is nauseating. One body goes by, deathly gray and covered in fungus. The male body is naked, and dark veins bulge under his skin. The man's head turns, and his bloodshot eyes lock with Hazen's. The man isn't dead after all, and he opens his mouth to scream with the most terrifying, inhuman shriek Hazen has ever heard. This awakens several of the other bodies in the container, and they turn reddened eyes to shriek at Hazen.

Hazen woke and sat upright with a small cry of fear. He was back in his hotel room, on his bed. Judging by the light coming through the window, it was early morning. He looked at his watch on the nightstand – 8:00 a.m. Someone had taken off his clothes, and he was now down to his boxers. He felt his brain sloshing inside his head, so he lay back on the pillows and held his face.

The door connecting to Renny's room opened, and Hazen had the presence of mind to pull the sheet over his bottom half. Renny, dressed in pajama shorts and a tank top, stepped across the room and sat cross-legged on the other side of the bed.

"You okay?"

"I forgot what a hangover feels like."

"There's water on your stand. And aspirin. I rubbed lotion on your latest tattoo. It looked sore."

"Thanks." Hazen looked over and reached for the water and aspirin. After swallowing the pills and taking a drink, he then lay back and looked at her. "Please, tell me you didn't have to undress me."

"Mino did that." Renny pulled her eyes from the tattoo of a futuristic car on his chest. She swallowed. "Your shirt was covered in blood."

Remembering Sonyeah's death, Hazen looked at the ceiling. "I feel awful."

"There's nothing you could've done."

He knew this was true, but even that was an odd feeling. "Did the cops find Vin?"

"No. But Seth talked to the cops after you gave your statement, and he told them he suspected who'd done this. The cops checked Sonyeah's phone, and Vin *did* call her right before she went outside. Then after we brought you back here..." Renny rubbed her arms and looked scared.

Hazen tried to sit up and made it as far as bracing himself on his elbows. "What? What's wrong now?"

Renny frowned. "Vin called Lhamo right after the cops left."

"What?" The volume of this hurt his head.

"Vin was gloating about how free he'll be with his vision partner dead. He said he's trying to get rid of the dream futures. He believes if he kills those of us who dream, only the nightmare versions will come true. He's trying to make them real, unalterable. Lhamo said he sounded like a madman."

Hazen felt his pulse racing. "Does that mean Vin's after you now too? And Oryan?"

Renny nodded. "Seth doesn't think we'll be safe in their community in Utah. Vin could get there easy. But if we stay on our own... Vin's seen us now. He'd find us."

Hazen sat all the way up. "So on top of everything else, now a psychopath is after us. What should we do, ask for protective custody?"

Renny raised an eyebrow at him. "You want to explain this to the cops?"

"No, you're right. I've been to the psych ward already." Hazen huffed. "Lhamo or Seth have any ideas?"

They're the only people who can help us, he thought.

Renny bit her lip. "Lhamo wants to take us to the Kota temple. Lhamo says Vin's never been there, and it's hard to get to. That'd probably be the best place to go. We can't abandon all this now. We can train at the temple, Lhamo says. We can write the prophecies there. And they say it's safe."

"Where's this temple?"

"Tibet."

He widened his eyes. "Tibet?"

"Yeah." She looked uncomfortable. "Problem is, the Kota don't have this kind of money to throw around. Lhamo paid for me to go to Toronto, but Tibet is a whole other load of moolah. He said he's not sure if the Kota have enough to pay for *him* to get to Tibet. If we're to go with him, the four of us will have to pay our own way."

"Renny, your life's in danger. I won't let a little thing like airfare hinder our escape."

"I can't let you pay for my-"

"Nonsense. Of course I will. You might've noticed by now that I'm a spoiled rich kid?"

"Well, the Maserati and private jet tipped me off."

Hazen had to smile. "How are Jazzmon and Oryan financially?"

"I don't know, but they looked pretty worried when Lhamo told us this problem."

"Guess I'm getting four tickets, then." Hazen realized something and rubbed his hands against his face. "Shit. I need to go home and ask for money."

"We can find another way..."

"No, I've *got* the money, Renny. That's not the problem."

"Then what is?"

"Any time I draw more than a thousand bucks from my accounts, I have to obtain written consent from one of my parents. That was one of the conditions my mom set in place when I was released from the hospital." Hazen looked away, embarrassed.

"Oh... And I'm guessing your mom wouldn't give consent for this?"

"Not a snowball's chance in Vegas. But I think I can talk my dad into it." He looked at Renny again. "He knows about my nightmares."

"What?" Her eyes widened. "I haven't told either of my parents, and they're *both* awesome. My brother doesn't even know."

"I wasn't exactly thinking clearly at the time." Hazen sighed. "My mom flipped out when I told her about seeing Chuck's accident, but my dad believed me that I wasn't making things up. He didn't understand what was going on, but he tried to talk my mom out of committing me. He didn't win the argument, obviously. When I was finally released, I was a mess for a while. In college, I got into...all kinds of things to avoid having nightmares."

Renny nodded. "Yeah, I remember a period where I didn't dream of you for a long time. I worried about you."

"Sorry." He hadn't even thought of this. "Anyway, when I finally cleaned up and sorted out how to avoid the distant-future nightmares, I started having the *usual* kinds of nightmares again. I couldn't keep it to myself anymore. I was visiting Dad for a weekend, and I told him about a nightmare of a lady drowning in Lake Michigan. He went with me to the lakeshore. Dad actually dove in and saved that lady."

Renny's eyes lit with memory. "Yeah, I saw that one. Never realized you told him, though."

"Ever since, Dad's believed me. Whenever I have a nightmare now, he lets me access my funds and travel to wherever I need to go. Mom thinks he's indulging my wanderlust – it's not like we can tell her the truth. Dad just tells her I'm traveling to find my way, which I suppose is partly true. And Dad knows I help people. After Chuck... It's cathartic for both of us, I think."

"Do you think he'll let you pay for *four* tickets to Tibet?"

"I hope so. This whole thing is kinda out there, though, so I'm not sure what to tell him."

Renny paused in thought. "You told me your mom's still in L.A. Where's your dad live?"

"Milwaukee, Wisconsin."

"Okay." Renny managed a smile. "Next stop, Milwaukee."

Hazen hesitated. "You don't need to come with me, Renny. It'd be safer to stay with Seth and the others. You guys can make plans, and I'll meet up with you once I've got the money."

Renny squirmed and crossed her arms, apparently not knowing what else to do with them. Then she rolled her eyes at herself. "Oh, hell. Hazen, I have to go. I've seen it."

"Seen what?"

"I had a dream right before I heard you cry out in here – I don't even want to know why." She held up a hand to stop him in case he wanted to tell her.

No, he thought, this is definitely not the time to tell her about those infected people.

"I dreamed of myself," said Renny, "with you, in a fancy house. I'm guessing that's your dad's place."

"Okay... Does Dad let us take the money?"

Renny made a face. "Didn't see that part." She stood from his bed and walked to the connecting door. "But I guess we'll find out together."

5

The Program Director

Hazen hadn't seen Renny this shy.

To be fair, Salvatore Stephenson was an intimidating figure. But the six foot five inch, gray haired, impeccably dressed man was smooth, and Hazen knew he could win over anyone. And, it was a fortunate bit of luck on his end that he'd suggested they have drinks in the library, where Renny would be at ease.

Accepting that he was off the wagon, Hazen sipped his Aberlour and grinned over his glass. They sat in leather chairs next to a grand fireplace, and the beautiful room was as pristine as ever. Renny was trying to listen to Sal – he insisted everyone call him that – talk about the latest developments at his branch of the World Space Program. But, Renny couldn't keep her gaze from drifting around the ceiling-high bookshelves.

"When they discovered new planets that might sustain human life, it prompted a resurgence of interest in space. The WSP's focus is finding a way to travel to..." Sal saw Renny was distracted and mistook it for boredom. "Sorry, I do tend to go on and on about the space program. It's such an exciting time."

Renny's head snapped back. "No, no. I'm sorry. It is interesting. I was admiring your collection of zombie fiction. It surprised me. You don't seem..." She didn't know where to go with this and looked to Hazen for help.

Hazen chuckled at her. "Dad's an eclectic guy."

Sal toasted him.

Hazen smiled. *This* was the parent he'd always known loved him. His mother was difficult, to put it mildly, but Hazen had always had a good relationship with his father.

"I may be a space nut," said Sal, "but I have my guilty pleasures. And I admit, the entertainment of my youth has always had a soft spot in my heart."

Renny smiled openly now. "I love millennial culture."

"It was a turbulent time, that's for sure. I still can't believe how much long-buried prejudice spilled back into the mainstream. But it did wake us up." Sal waved a hand to move on. "As for the more enjoyable aspects of the culture, I'm admittedly a nerdy fan."

Renny rolled her eyes. "My mom named me after an actor who was on *one* episode of a sci-fi show she liked."

"Ha! Our parents gave us weird names too, but we hipsters took it to a whole new level."

"Yes! It's like a competition to see who can be more ridiculously inventive."

Sal laughed and pointed at Hazen. "I picked his name because his mother wouldn't let me name him Raison!"

Hazen looked at the ceiling.

Renny burst out laughing.

Sal looked pleased with himself and took a gulp from his whiskey.

Hazen looked between them. "Do I even need to be here?"

"Sorry, Raison."

Renny lost it again.

Sal turned back to his son more seriously. "Where've you been gallivanting this time?"

Hazen restarted the conversation he'd tried an hour ago when they first sat down. "I was in Toronto. That's where I met Renny. Then we flew to Vegas."

Sal's eyes widened. "Did you two elope? And you didn't even tell-"

"No!" Hazen felt himself blush, and he slapped his face. "That's not what I meant. We were-"

Renny laughed, then looked at Hazen and contemplated his face. "You know, Hazen does look a lot like that famous singer my mom loved. I always thought he was cute."

"Oh, good grief." Hazen pinched between his eyes.

Sal took another sip and held up his hands to settle the room. "Okay, I'm sorry. No more jokes at your expense, son. It's not every day you bring a beautiful woman home."

Renny looked surprised by this and lifted an eyebrow at Hazen.

He ignored her and plowed ahead. "Dad, we went to Vegas because Renny wanted me to meet people there. They're called the Kota."

Sal's expression flashed with concern. "That new cult?"

"What? No. Dad they're not-"

"Sir," Renny interjected, "I grew up as Baptist as Baptist can be. There's nothing about the Kota movement that makes me think they're a cult. My parents even approved of my going on a Kota mission trip during college."

"Baptist, huh?" Sal's eyes went to her nose ring. "I doubt your parents approve of that little guy."

"I said I *grew up* Baptist. Then I realized it wasn't evil to have fun." A smirk pulled at the corner of her mouth. "But my style choices don't bother my parents. They were much more upset about my MFA in Creative Writing. 'Useless' was the exact word they used." She winked at Hazen. "I'll show them."

Hazen made a face. "Anyway, we met with the Kota because... Dad, they know about people like me."

Sal lowered his half-raised glass, and his gaze swung to Renny.

This is our big, weird family secret, thought Hazen. Can't blame him for being surprised I'd talk about it in front of her.

"Dad, Renny's like me too."

Sal looked at her.

All her laughter gone now, Renny nodded back at him.

"So..." Sal tried to piece this together. "The Kota can explain why you have these nightmares? Can they make them stop?"

"No, I don't think so. But they say there's a reason for what I see. If they can help me figure out why I see visions, I want to go with them."

"Where?"

"Tibet."

"Have you lost your mind?" Sal's face paled. "I'm sorry. I didn't mean..."

"It's okay, Dad. I'm not crazy. I know that for sure now." He smiled at Renny, then took a breath. "Dad, I need to do this. And I don't mean this is some selfish quest to find myself or anything – although that's probably what we should tell Mom. Renny and I can use our visions to potentially help a lot of people."

Sal thought a moment. "But you're already helping people. Isn't that enough? I've never understood your nightmares, and I'm sorry I can't. I really wish I could've helped you sort out all this. Especially after losing Charles."

Hazen swallowed. "I know, Dad."

Sal set his drink on a side table. Then he stood from his seat and smoothed out the front of his suit shirt. "Miss Nado, would you mind if we excuse ourselves? I'd like to have a word alone with my son."

Renny held her glass and smiled up at him. "Of course, sir. I'll stay here and look at your books if that's okay?"

"My books would be honored." Sal winked at her. Then he motioned for Hazen to join him as he left the room.

Hazen rose, swallowed the rest of his drink, and looked at Renny.

She made an exaggerated scared face before smiling. "Go. I'm sure you'll be fine."

Hazen took a breath and hurried after his father, who'd exited into the hall. Sal led him onto a moonlit deck off the back of the enormous house. They stood together against the far rail, which overlooked a hilly drop to a rocky beach. Lake Michigan lapped against the rocks, and the moonlight created flashing waves of silver from here to the dark horizon.

"Hazen, did something happen? When you first showed up, you both looked horribly nervous, like you were scared. Are you running from something?"

Damn it, thought Hazen. He's always so perceptive.

He put his hands in his pockets. "Can what happened in Vegas stay there? I don't know how to explain. This is all...surreal."

Sal frowned. "I don't like this. Are you sure you can trust these Kota people? I understand you want answers, but Tibet's a long way from home."

"I know, but I need to do this. I'm not a child, and I can take care of myself. I *am* going to Tibet. I'll find a way to get us there even if you refuse to let me get the money." He looked across the water, then back at his father. "You trust me to know what I'm doing, don't you? You have so far, and I've told you some pretty weird stuff."

Sal looked over at him, his face shadowed. "Yes, I believe in you, Hazen. But I'm your father, and I want to keep you safe – that was true the day you were born, it's true now that you're thirty, and it'll be true 'til the day I die. And you're a special case, since you have this *thing* in your life that I don't understand. It frightens me."

"It frightens me too. But I learned years ago not to run from it. And now I have people counting on me."

Sal sighed. "Are you sure you won't consider coming to work for me at the WSP? You're good with people – you'd fit perfectly with our international relations team."

"I can't, Dad. I appreciate everything you've done for me. I really do. Without your success, I couldn't help people the way I do. But I have to do what *I* do, not what you do."

"But why go to the other side of the world? Aren't there enough people in our own country who need help? We have poverty, corruption, disease, famine. You've had tons of visions of people *here*, right? Why can't you stay here, find a fulfilling day job, and play hero on the side?"

Hazen thought on the future he'd seen.

"There's more I'm meant to do, Dad. I can't explain it, but the Kota can help me learn what I'm supposed to do for the future."

Sal held the rail. "Isn't the present enough to fix? The future isn't always your responsibility, son."

But this one might be, thought Hazen. The present world has problems, yes. But the future I see is going to be worse. So. Much. Worse. If I'm meant to somehow make it better, I can't ignore that responsibility. I've tried to heal hundreds of short-term futures, but the distant-future visions have always felt more important. *That* future is the world I have to care about.

"Dad, I need to go to Tibet. Please, understand." He made a face. "Renny's going too. At least she'll be there to watch after me, right?"

Sal half-grinned at this. He took a second, then finally nodded. "Okay. I'll go with you to the bank in the morning." He put a hand on Hazen's shoulder and smiled. "But I get to drive your car while you're gone. The service brought it back from the airport last night."

Hazen smiled. "Deal."

6

The WSP Ship

Several months later, Hazen woke to the sound of his tent swelling and contracting with the wind. He'd grown accustomed to the sound, and to rains which bounced off his tent's cover. As he sat up from his pile of blankets, he stretched to relieve muscles stiff from sleeping on the single mat. He took a deep breath of thin, cool air and reached for his black robes to dress.

When Hazen stepped out of his tent, he looked first beyond the stone wall of the Kota temple. The scattered clouds above allowed bright sunlight to shine upon Gyantse's high hill nearby. A Tibetan monastery stood atop this hill of dirt and stone, and red walls bordered the hilltop like a crown. Far in the distance, gray-blue mountains stretched across the horizon. If standing outside the temple walls, Hazen knew one could see the surrounding land's greens and blues and browns, washed out with a hazy gray the farther one looked. There was also the highway that had brought them from Lhasa over the rivers and valleys and overall gorgeous scenery.

It's a beautiful land, thought Hazen. There's something quiet, holy, and completely foreign about this place. It's intimidating. We're so far from *everything*... But the locals in Gyantse are kind. And the Kota have taught us so much.

He turned to see the neighboring tents of his three friends. Jazzmon, also wearing black robes, had just emerged from hers. She hadn't been thrilled at first about cutting her hair as short as Renny's, and even now Hazen saw her stroke the unfamiliar buzz cut. When she noticed Hazen, they exchanged bows. Then Jazzmon headed off for her morning routine.

This practice of silence thing is killing me, thought Hazen. I don't know how Mino does this. At least we get to talk after noon.

He looked at the other two tents, but there was no movement from inside.

Renny and Oryan are probably already at chores, thought Hazen. Glad *I* don't have cow duty today.

He smiled and walked around their tents to the main section of the Kota temple. The locals of Gyantse had sold the Kota this land over a decade ago. The humble, white-gray, stone buildings were a good hike from town, but the Kota had worked hard to be respectful of the surrounding culture. The main, single-story building was shaped like an 'L' with a narrow porch of wood lining the inward-facing walls. Hazen walked over the bare ground to this porch and paused to look over by the stables.

Renny and Oryan, dressed in black robes, were indeed at work with the livestock. Oryan was leading Betsy by her halter toward the temple's gate, presumably taking her to pasture. Renny looked up from tugging on Otto's lead and spotted Hazen watching her, and she stuck out her tongue.

Hazen laughed silently and turned to enter the temple, slipping off his shoes at the door. The front room was warm from a fireplace in the far wall. A visitor had long ago gifted the temple with a thick, red carpet. In its center stood a low table surrounded by floor pillows. On either side of this communal room, hallways led to the monks' quarters, library, kitchen, wash rooms, training rooms, rooms for meditation, and the sensory deprivation chamber (not his favorite).

Making his way first to the simple kitchen, Hazen found an elderly woman in black robes preparing her breakfast. He recognized her as Mino's sister, who like many at the temple spoke little English. The head-shaved nun smiled with a small bow and continued her activities with a grace Hazen always admired. He himself tried not to clack his pan and bowl as he prepared tsampa porridge over the rudimentary stove. When he was finished, he poured himself warm tea from the communal pot, smiled at Mino's sister, and carried his meal back out to the front room's table. She joined him a short time later and sat across from him.

Renny's right, he thought. The Kota use such a jumble of religious and cultural traditions. They've tried to adapt to the surrounding culture to make locals welcome. They've adopted things like these robes, shaving our heads...bowing. And they call those who study here monks and nuns, but those are just the terms that make the most sense. Lhamo says the Kota faith is what matters. As long as that's the foundation, each Kota community around the world is allowed to live however they feel comfortable. That's pretty cool. I wonder what a Kota community in L.A. would look like. Maybe I'll start one someday and invite my mom.

He grinned at this thought, imagining her reaction if he showed up as he was dressed now.

When finished breaking his fast, Hazen cleaned his dishes and headed down a hall to the meditation rooms. He entered the one set aside for him, slid the wooden door closed, and knelt on the mat in the darkness. By memory, he reached for the candle and struck a match, illuminating the tiny, stone room. With the candle lit in front of him, he cleared his mind as Lhamo had trained him.

Seth and Lhamo had been right about how their visions would change. It'd been months since Hazen or the others saw their normal nightmares or dreams. Instead, now every vision showed them the distant future. And the visions were clearer. Stronger. What each of them saw still didn't make sense alone, but together they were able to piece together what they were seeing.

Breathe, he thought. Hear the stillness. Become weightless. Let the vision come...

The candle light blurred as Hazen stared at it.

He stands in a thousand different places at once, yet they're all the same place. Whenever the scene changes, it's only the time of the place that changes. He suddenly stands in a living room, and a swirl of red and yellow light is before him. He makes a motion with his hand that triggers the anomaly. He's then floating in a place where only the light exists. It seems eternal. Swirling hues of red mix around him and pulse in and out, acting as the heartbeat of this realm. Different openings appear before him. As he floats over the lights, he sees that these openings look into many exotic lands and places.

Hazen's open eyes blinked as he came out of the vision. He sucked in a breath. Looking at the candle in front of him, he saw it was half-melted.

How much time was I out? he thought.

He blew out the candle and rose from the mat, then turned and slid open the door. His eyes adjusted to the light as he walked up the temple hall, and when he came into the communal front room he saw his three friends already gathered. It was after noon, surely, but they still were silent as they tended to their individual tasks. Renny had her usual notebook open in front of her, and at least ten separate pieces of paper were organized around her on the tabletop. She stared down at whatever she was writing while tapping her pen against her teeth. Oryan had taken a piece of paper from Renny, and he drew with one hand while eating a piece of dried yak meat in the other. His ears stuck out now that his hair was shaved, and his glasses made his head look small as Hazen walked by him. Jazzmon also had paper and was writing fast.

Looks like she had a vision, thought Hazen. And Oryan always draws what he sees, so he must've dreamed too. Good.

While the visions they had now were stronger and clearer, they were also fewer. In a way, this was a sign of their progress. Over the months, they'd pieced together several dreams and nightmares and made sense of what they were shown. After much debate about wording, Renny would then write the final version of what they'd seen, thusly recording prophecies of these future events. They'd so far created half a dozen prophecies. The interesting discovery they'd made was that, if they weren't sure about the wording, they'd keep having visions pertaining to that prophecy until they got it right. Once Renny's final version was apparently satisfactory to fate, the visions of those events would cease.

Hazen sat at the table beside Renny, across from Oryan and Jazzmon. He looked down at his bare arm and saw his Mark tattoo.

We're trying to solidify the Mark Prophecy, he thought. I hope one of the others had a vision about it, because I think mine was something new. I didn't sense any of the Marked... It was like I was a person I've never envisioned before.

He didn't want to be the one to break the silence, so he looked over to read the paper nearest him.

'The Virus
When the mind of man abuses all known by him
and calamity comes most unnatural,
the sons of men shall be tested.
Some will revolt from truth;
others faithful will remain.
Only the true Kota, the un-tainted,
shall escape the curse of man's corruption.'

Those visions I certainly don't miss, thought Hazen. The infected people always gave me the creeps. Floating in those containers. Terrorizing city streets. Attacking soldiers who tried to put them down. And always that horrible sense of being out of my mind. Enraged. Hungry...

He looked at Jazzmon where she'd finished writing and was reading over her paper.

Jazzmon has nightmares about scientists, he thought. She feels their greed and corruption. They don't care about the infected. And she said they do horrible experiments on people, cutting into them...

He felt a chill and watched Oryan drawing across from him.

The other two are lucky, he thought. Their dreams sound so much nicer. They see tons of Kota in the future. Our people stand up against greed and corruption. And while Jazzmon and I see the virus spreading from people to people, Renny says the Kota remain unharmed. She felt like they escape. And *how* they escape... Oryan dreamed of Kota loading onto a futuristic spacecraft.

Hazen's gaze moved from paper to paper until he found the prophecy he wanted.

'The Signal
When all arrives,
time shall be opened.
Heaven's churning lights will be key –
a sign unto the Kota.
Through the doorway they shall pass,
but some knowing truth will remain behind.
Hope will come for Earth's side of the gateway.'

This is talking about those lights we always see, he thought. They're these 'churning lights.' And if we're right, the lights show us a realm that's never been opened before. But where are the Kota going in their spacecraft? This Signal of the lights opening means 'time' is opening. Where does this doorway lead? To some new future? To the past? That certainly makes sense with my new vision just now.

He thought back on his vision with these churning lights.

That was the least like a nightmare I've ever had, he thought. I mean, it was terrifying to not know if I could control it... But it was kind of awesome too.

Oryan let out a long breath, finally breaking the silence. "Okay, Renny, what are we pretty sure about so far on the Mark Prophecy?"

She read the paper in front of her, ignoring the crossed off lines and notes in the margins.

"'The Mark
By the Bearers brought into time,
fulfillment shall come in a Mark,
and hope in four children born.'"

She tapped a line with her pen. "And the part we're not sure about is... 'The enemy will disappear when the four Marked win.'"

Hazen leaned his elbows on the table. "Yeah, that doesn't feel right."

The others seemed to agree. And since they still had visions about the Mark Prophecy, fate didn't seem to like this wording either.

Oryan twirled his pencil. "Okay, so what'd everyone see today?"

Jazzmon wiggled on her floor pillow and made a face. "Why don't you dreamers go first?"

"Hmm." Oryan read his vision partner's expression. "Start with the good news. Got it." He motioned to Renny. "Lady's first."

Hazen smiled to himself. He liked Oryan. Jazzmon wasn't half as much fun, though Hazen understood why, considering the things she saw.

Renny took a breath. "I dreamed I was looking down at a newborn little girl, and I turned her to see the Mark on her arm." She shrugged. "I've seen that dream lots of times since my visions started. I think I'm always the same man, looking down at the baby in my manly arms." She smirked.

Oryan pointed at her with his pencil. "And do you get a feeling like everything's coming together? Like the girl with the Mark is an answer to prayer?"

"Yes, exactly. There's this remarkable sense of hope. And accomplishment."

After a twirl of his pencil, Oryan tapped it on the table. "I had a repeat dream too. Just like yours, except I was holding a Marked little boy. My dreams give me manly arms too, by the way."

Hazen laughed.

Jazzmon looked at Oryan. "Since you draw so well, it's a shame you never see the man's face. You could draw him, and in the future the Kota could use the drawing to find the Bearer and know exactly who will father these children."

Hazen looked at the papers on the table, but the Bearers Prophecy was on the far side of Renny.

Oryan tucked his pencil behind his ear. "Yeah, that'd help. But if we're seeing through future people's eyes, it makes sense that we see only what they're looking at. I mean, it always drives me nuts in movies when people have back-flashes and see themselves." He waved with his hands. "If you're supposed to be seeing something from your own memory, how the heck does it make sense that you see yourself from different camera angles?"

Renny and Hazen laughed.

Jazzmon even grinned at this. "If you had a repeat dream, then what's your new drawing?"

Oryan spun the paper around and pushed it to the middle of the table so they could see. "I was redrawing what I remembered from my dream about the Signal Prophecy. I wasn't happy with the last drawing."

Hazen looked at this update and saw a spacecraft similar to the original drawing. But Oryan had been less hurried in this drawing, and his lines and details were clearer.

"Holy..." Hazen spun the drawing to face him. "I know this ship."

"From a nightmare?"

"No. I've seen sketches of a ship almost exactly like this in my dad's study."

Oryan's jaw dropped. "Oh, man. I forgot how cool your dad's job is."

Jazzmon tried to refocus her partner. "You're sure this spacecraft takes Kota through one of the churning portals?"

"Positive."

Jazzmon looked at Hazen. "If it's a World Space Program ship and one you've seen planned..."

Hazen knew what she was thinking. "This future might not be as distant as we think."

This was the first hint they'd had of a timeline. It left Hazen with a weird feeling.

Oryan twirled his pencil and looked at Jazzmon. "Alright, out with it. What was your nightmare?"

The Dane took a breath and looked down at her notes to guide her. "I didn't *see* anything. But I might've been in a ship, because I heard engines firing and I felt claustrophobic. I was more terrified than I'd ever been in my life. I felt like I was weighed down with...darkness. Like with a shadow. I sensed someone's hate but couldn't separate it from my own feelings. And I heard a man shouting. He was furious. He was yelling, 'They're following us! Do you think they know we have the virus?' Then he started swearing and muttering. I heard engines firing, and I got the feeling like we were accelerating into space." She shrugged. "That's it. Not real helpful or easy to interpret, I know."

Weird one, thought Hazen.

Jazzmon looked at him hopefully. "Did your nightmare offer any clarification?"

"No." Hazen crossed his arms atop the table. "My vision didn't have anything to do with the Mark Prophecy." He told them about entering the fiery lights and exploring different times and places. "I don't know who I was. I was terrified but also really excited. It was one of the weirdest visions I've ever had. But I didn't sense anything about the Marked." He gave Jazzmon a sympathetic smile. "Sorry, but guess your nightmare's the last new vision we're getting about the Mark Prophecy."

Oryan whistled. "So we're finishing one prophecy and starting a new one all in the same day. Awesome."

Renny tapped her pen on everything she'd written as they talked. "But how do we interpret Jazzmon's dream? What does it change or add from our earlier guess about this last line?"

"Which was what again?" asked Hazen.

"'The enemy will disappear when the four Marked win.'"

Jazzmon leaned an elbow on the table and trailed a finger through her stubbled hair, thinking. "That interpretation is what this felt like. I was seeing from the side of the enemy. And the mood was intense. It was like a great battle had just happened, and my side lost."

Renny studied what she'd recorded. "You said the man yelled, 'They're following us! Do you think they know we have the virus?'"

"Yes." Jazzmon nodded and looked at her own writings. "And I think 'they' is the Marked."

"It has to be the Marked, right?" said Oryan. "They're the heroes of our dreams." He grinned at how corny this sounded.

"So," Hazen thought aloud, "maybe the part we have wrong is the enemy disappearing. It's more like they're running away, and the Marked are following. Could that be right?"

Jazzmon was thinking again. "They're *fleeing*. That word feels more right."

Renny wrote 'fleeing' on the Mark Prophecy paper.

The Dane frowned. "I'm also not sure about focusing on these enemies. My whole nightmare was clouded in intensity and fear, but when the man talked about having the virus, I felt this horrible sense of evil. I think the virus is what we should focus on, not whoever these enemies are."

Renny wrote 'evil' on the Mark Prophecy paper and circled it.

Hazen agreed, thinking back on his nightmares from the Virus Prophecy. "All along, it's been like the virus is the greatest evil of the future. It destroys humanity. The Kota are meant to escape from it. And if the Marked are supposed to bring hope to Earth..."

"That must mean the Marked save Earth from the virus," Renny finished.

"Yes," said Jazzmon with a nod. "That feels right. It's not 'the enemy will disappear when the four Marked win.' It's more like the virus is this terrible evil, and it's using the men in the ship to flee Earth to get away from the Marked, who are following. There's a sense that this isn't over, too, so maybe leave it open-ended somehow." She smiled at Renny. "Can you make that sound better?"

Renny nodded and wrote for a few minutes, scratching words out a few times. "Okay, how about this?

"'The Mark
By the Bearers brought into time,
fulfillment shall come in a Mark,
and hope in four children born.
Evil will flee Earth before the four Marked.'"

Jazzmon nodded. "That's good."

They all seemed to relax, and Hazen smiled at Renny, feeling proud of his vision partner once again.

Oryan stood from his floor pillow. "Well, I'm starving."

Jazzmon also rose. "I said I'd help Seth in the gardens this afternoon, but I'd also like a quick lunch first."

Renny started packing up her various papers. "Okay, see you guys later."

The other vision partners bowed out of habit and left the temple.

Hazen stood and helped Renny reach Oryan's drawing to tuck in her notebook. "Need help with anything?"

"Nope. I'm just going to throw this notebook in the library and then take a bath." She wrinkled her nose. "Being a cowgirl is not as fun as I expected."

Hazen grinned. "Okay. See you later?"

"Later, partner." Renny used Seth's southern twang as she said this. She smiled up at Hazen. "Or, more accurately... Later, vision partner."

Hazen laughed and walked to the exit to retrieve his shoes.

Later that evening, Hazen stretched his legs as he sat on a hillside overlooking the twinkling city of Gyantse. From here he could see the more modern streets where tourists stayed, and he could also see the older sections of town. The impressive monastery on the mountainous hill was, as always, the dominant feature. Above, Hazen had never seen a sky so clear.

He heard someone panting up the steep trail. Looking over, he saw Renny as she held up the end of her robes and watched her footing on the loose dirt. Under her robes, she'd put on one of the black, long-sleeve shirts they'd bought in Lhasa for colder weather. Since she was watching the ground so intently, Hazen raised a hand in case she hadn't spotted him.

"Hey." She panted as she came to share his boulder seat. She laughed at herself. "I'm so tired from hauling those cows out this morning."

He smiled. "It's hard because of the oxygen. I was panting too."

Renny faced the open scenery below them. "I had a dream. Thought I should come tell you right away."

"Do tell."

"Well, you know the Bearers Prophecy about the chosen brothers who'll guide the Marked. We've sorted out that the brothers will stay on Earth after the Kota go through the swirling portal to escape the virus.

'The Bearers
The remnant, remaining to reveal the light, must strive on.
Hope will come, as vowed by heaven.
Through preservation, time shall hold the chosen brothers.
The one will seed;
the other will foster.
And so, both shall bear.'"

Hazen nodded.

Renny looked at the horizon of mountains. "Oryan and I keep seeing the father, so he must be the brother who will 'seed.' I'm wondering if your vision earlier was of the other brother."

Hazen raised an eyebrow.

"My dream," she said, "was also super weird. But I think I was seeing through the eyes of the same man you were. He could open the realm of the lights. He was standing in a living room like the one you described, and he made a motion with his hand that opened a portal. It looked so cool."

He nodded with a smile, remembering the same.

"In my dream, the man watched the one little boy with a Mark as the kid played in a sandbox. He felt proud of the kid, but it wasn't the same feeling I get from the boy's dad. I think that means it was the other brother, the boy's uncle."

This made sense.

Renny sighed. "It was amazing, the things I saw him doing. He could *change* history, Hazen. We know the lights' realm has something to do with time, so if he can access the lights, it makes sense that he can fiddle with time." She made a face. "I'm not using 'fiddle' in this prophecy. It was more like he altered things. But it wasn't just for fun. He had a deep sense of purpose. He was...*interceding* to change history in ways that help people. I think I'll call him the Interceder."

"Yeah, that fits with what I felt too."

"He's so powerful, right? But he's also lonely. It was his job to do all this, but..."

Hazen watched her face and saw her usual expression whenever she was trying to choose the right words.

"He alone will do the work," she said, "and he will do the work alone."

Hazen smiled. "I can't wait to see more of this guy."

They paused to look out at the mountains. The breeze grew cooler, and Hazen knew soon the sun would drop. Then they'd be freezing. But he didn't want to leave just yet. Renny seemed to be of the same mind, and she put her head on his shoulder. This surprised him a little, but it didn't bother him. Not at all...

"You know," she said, "if we really have finalized the Mark Prophecy, we'll stop seeing visions of the Marked when they're young. I'll miss seeing those kids."

He smiled. "Me too."

Though I always saw scarier things around them, he thought.

"Renny, do you think everything will work out? What if we miss something? What do *any* of us know about interpreting visions? We're guessing."

"But everything's clearer since the four of us came together."

"Yeah...but you guys vetoed me about writing the prophecies *exactly* like we see them. Shouldn't we be precise so those in the future know what to expect, who to involve, and what to do? I know you're having fun writing the prophecies and being all poetic and mysterious, but that seems dangerous considering how serious this future seems to be."

"Except that we don't know how to interpret *exactly* what we're seeing. If we wrote everything as fact when we actually can't possibly know everything – we're seeing the distant future, after all – that could be bad too."

"Except if the Kota leave in that WSP ship, this isn't so distant after all."

Renny sighed heavily into his shoulder. "I'm not worried. The Signal Prophecy is at the beginning of everything, and I'm guessing there's lots of time between then and everything with the Marked." She squeezed his arm. "We have time to understand what these prophecies mean, Hazen. Fate seems happy with how we've worded them, so that's good enough for me. What's important is that we get them written now, while the visions still come."

"I know. I just hate this responsibility. The more we see and the more we write, the more confusing it gets." He frowned. "This is too much responsibility for four people."

Renny chuckled. "That's probably what the four Marked children will think. At least *we* don't have to save the world."

"No, we only have to tell them how to do it."

She sighed again. "Well, if we're nearing the end of our visions, our part in this will be done soon. I'll finally hand over all my notes to Lhamo, he can start the translating process for monks of the future, and after that we can all go home."

What then? thought Hazen.

"You're right. Sorry I'm such a downer." He kissed the top of her head in a quick peck. "Come on, let's go. It's getting late, and we don't want to freeze up here."

She sat up. "Okay. I'm starving, anyway."

He laughed and followed her to the trail. "You eat more than I do!"

"Well, Mino had me fasting yesterday. Of course, I'm starving. And you can't tell me you're not sick of highland barley in *everything*."

He stepped over a pointy rock. "I'm more sick of the air-dried mutton. I'd kill for a thick, juicy burger."

"If you make me dream of burgers tonight, I'll kill you."

Hazen laughed and hurried down the trail.

7

The False Prophet

The next morning, Hazen woke to screaming. Real screaming. He sat up from his mat and saw shadows of people running by his tent. They were shouting to each other in the local language he didn't know, but he heard the panic in their voices.

A gunshot blasted from the direction of the temple, and Hazen winced.

After scrambling out of his blankets, he looked down at his tattooed body. He wore only boxers, but there was no time to dress in his robes. Sliding into his shoes, he flipped open the tent flap and exited into the freezing air.

Monks and nuns ran screaming and shouting from the main yard that stretched in front of the temple. They hurried by Hazen, seeking shelter.

"Renny!"

Hazen stooped to open her tent flap, but she wasn't there. He next went to Jazzmon's tent, then Oryan's with the same results. More monks ran around the corner of the temple, and Hazen saw they looked absolutely terrified.

Against any natural instinct, Hazen ran where the crowds were fleeing from. He turned into the front yard of the temple and saw monks running to the stables to hide. Still more monks and nuns hurried in the opposite direction into the temple doors, none taking the time to remove their shoes. Once enough of them had cleared the yard, Hazen saw the source of their fear.

A brown-haired, thin, tall man in European clothes stood in the center of the yard. He held a gun pointed at Oryan and Renny, who looked like they'd been working in the stables.

No, thought Hazen. Oh, God!

A breeze blew, reminding him he was half-naked, but he fought off a shiver and took a slow step forward. The man had his back to Hazen. If he could sneak all the way across the yard...

Renny, her face tense with fear, saw Hazen around the man. She returned her eyes to the stranger between them so she didn't give Hazen away. He couldn't see Oryan's face, since the stranger was equally tall. Then Hazen noticed something burning on the ground in front of them.

"You're Vin, aren't you?" said Oryan.

"Indeed I am!" Vin didn't seem to care who heard him, and he waved his free arm while he spoke like they were old friends. "And hello to you, dreamer! It's taken me a really long time to find you guys, hasn't it?"

The yard was clear now, but Hazen saw monks peeking out from the stables. He took another step and checked his footing for anything that would make noise if he stepped on it. Bumps covered his skin, but he held his mouth closed so his teeth didn't chatter.

"What..." Oryan had his hands up, and Hazen heard the fright in his friend's voice. "What do you want?"

Vin giggled. "That's what Lhamo asked right before I shot him. Renny, you should know Lhamo tried to talk me out of taking your book. He put up a good fight, but..." Vin motioned to the small fire between them.

The prophecies! thought Hazen. All Renny's notes!

The notebook was little more than black char now, a few flames still licking the pages.

"What do you want?" asked Oryan again.

Hazen then realized that his friend had spotted him approaching. Oryan was trying to keep Vin distracted.

"I'm on a mission to get rid of you dreamers, obviously. I've seen so many fun things since Sonyeah's been gone. I'm thinking..." He scratched his head with the gun before quickly pointing it back at Oryan, then Renny. "I'm thinking that if I get rid of *all* you dreamers, the happy endings won't exist anymore! Then I can control the things I see in my nightmares!"

He's a lunatic, thought Hazen as he took another step.

Renny was trying to be brave. "Don't do this."

Vin aimed the gun at her, then at Oryan, then at Renny. "I'll do whatever I want!" He jumped up and down as he shouted, "I am the true prophet!"

And with that, he shot Oryan in the heart.

"No!"

The scream came from the temple entrance, and Hazen looked to see Jazzmon in the doorway. Seth grabbed her from behind and pulled her back inside for cover.

"Ha!" Vin kept the gun on Renny but looked at the temple now with a wide smile. "Seth, was that you? Why don't you come say, hello?"

Wind swept over the silence that followed this.

"Well, that's just rude!"

Seth's voice called from the temple, "Let them go, Vin. This won't accomplish anything."

"Oh, that's where you're wrong! I-" Vin saw Hazen in his periphery and backed up to keep the gun on Renny while also able to watch his challenger now.

Shit, thought Hazen.

"Hello, fellow nightmare-er! A bit underdressed for these parts, aren't you?"

Hazen stopped where he stood and lifted his hands. Despite the cold, he felt himself sweating. "Vin, don't do this. We can get you help."

"Help? I don't need help. That's the whole point. I want control. I'm trying to liberate you too, you know! You and Jazzmon. If I get rid of your dreamers, you won't have to see alterable futures anymore! You'll see only the real future, like me!"

Hazen answered carefully. "No, thank you."

"You think I came here without seeing how this all plays out? I *will* kill the dreamers, Hazen. I've already got Jazzmon's." Vin motioned to Oryan's body as if his point wasn't clear. Then he motioned with the gun to Renny. "Once you're free of her, you can have more visions and then go watch it happen in real life!" He winked. "Or, you know, help it out a bit. That's pretty fun too."

Renny was looking at Hazen, crying. She mouthed, 'I love you,' which was almost more than Hazen could take.

Don't believe Vin, he thought. Please, don't believe him. This has to be alterable!

Vin looked at Renny. "You're the writer, yeah? Don't you think it's so cliché that the girl always has to die to teach the guy a lesson?" With a smirk, he aimed the gun at Renny's head.

"No!" Hazen's body moved forward before he knew what he was doing.

Suddenly a loud, strong voice shouted from the stables. "Vin!"

Vin, moving fast, spun to face whoever addressed him. He pointed the gun at Hazen, causing him to slide to a stop and lift his hands. Vin then moved the gun back and forth between Renny and Hazen.

Mino, who'd only this moment broken his vow of silence, stepped out of the stable. The pudgy monk held a shotgun aimed at Vin, and he stepped forward to stand in the yard a few body lengths from Vin.

Vin scoffed. "Mino? Really? Everyone here knows you aren't going to shoot-"

Mino fired, hitting Vin square in the chest. The tall man fell backward to the dirt. His head rolled to face Hazen, but his eyes never blinked again.

Several hiding monks emerged at once and ran to Oryan's body to check him. Mino held his gun at the ready and checked Vin, kicking the gun from the man's hand.

"Renny!"

Hazen ran to her as she slumped to sit on the ground. He knelt beside her, his whole body numb with cold now, and pulled her into a hug. She shook in his arms.

Jazzmon ran out of the temple and pushed monks aside to reach Oryan. When she stood over him and saw he was for sure dead, her face twisted and she sank to her knees to cry over him.

Seth arrived to the small crowd. He put a hand on Mino's shoulder before coming to the prophets.

Renny sniffed and looked up at him. "Lhamo? Is he really dead? That first shot we heard..."

With a single nod, Seth glared over at Vin's corpse.

Hazen looked where someone had accidentally kicked the black remains of Renny's notebook.

Was this all for nothing? he thought.

Jazzmon continued to wail.

8

The...

Two weeks later, Hazen stood with an arm around Renny as they watched a jeep drive off with Jazzmon. An urn was tied to the roof of the jeep. Without argument, Seth had allowed Jazzmon to use Gyantse's local phone bar and make travel arrangements. She was taking Oryan's remains home to their Kota community in Scandinavia.

The three remaining prophets had parted with promises to stay in touch, but Hazen doubted Jazzmon would want to remember what had happened here.

This whole prophet thing works in partners, thought Hazen. I still have Renny, thank God. But Jazzmon must feel so alone... I'll have to keep tabs on her. She's a fellow nightmare-er, after all. Either of us could turn into Vin.

Renny wiped a tear. "Have you still had no visions?"

"No. Not a single one. You?"

She shook her head and watched the jeep as it grew smaller and smaller down the highway.

They weren't sure what the sudden stop of visions meant. None of them had had a vision since Oryan's death. Renny and Hazen had talked about this while Jazzmon kept to herself, and they were sure their work wasn't finished.

Hazen looked along the temple walls and saw no one nearby. He lowered his voice just the same. "I know you recited the prophecies for Seth to officially record, but did you tell him about your new Interceder dream?"

"No, I haven't said anything to anyone. I never even wrote about it in the book Vin burned, so even Lhamo didn't know. Lhamo probably read what I recorded about *your* Interceder vision, but... Well, he'll never tell anyone either." She swallowed and looked freshly saddened.

Hazen kissed her forehead. "Come on. Seth wanted to see us once Jazzmon left."

They walked back through the temple gate. A vulture cried above as it flew from the mountains, and Hazen wondered if this was a scavenger who'd picked at Vin's remains. The Kota had given him a sky burial on the side of a mountain, leaving his body to return to nature any way it pleased.

It's a creepy ancient custom, thought Hazen, but practical. And none of us wanted to give Vin a funeral, anyway. Let the birds have him.

He decided not to point out the vulture to Renny.

They walked into the temple and to the library, where Seth had told them to meet. It was a small room, much smaller than Hazen's father's study. But it was cozy, with a few soft chairs to sit in and a desk from which Lhamo had conducted Kota business. Now Seth sat at this desk, looking at mail collected from Gyantse. Books lay open on the table, all in a language Hazen couldn't read.

Seth looked weary as he lifted his head to see them enter. "How are you both?"

"Okay," said Renny.

Hazen shrugged.

"Hmm." Seth leaned back in the wooden chair. "Mino and I have talked. We don't feel it's right to keep you here anymore now that your visions have stopped. And we thought we were keeping you safe here, but..."

Hazen scowled. "Are you kicking us out?"

"No. You're welcome to stay if you wish, but you should be free to go home. Be young and in love while you can."

Hazen blushed and glanced at Renny to see her looking anywhere but at him.

Seth grinned and changed the subject by patting a notebook on the desk. "Renny, I'll be eternally grateful for your good memory. We'll translate these prophecies and have the monks make as many copies as they can. The prophecies won't be lost again, I promise you."

Renny took a breath and nodded. "Glad I could help."

Hazen frowned. "What if our visions start back up? Should we come back?"

"You're of course welcome back any time. But you told us before that with every prophecy you recorded, you had fewer and fewer visions. Maybe they've stopped now not only because one of your partners was lost. Maybe the prophecies are simply...finished."

It took every bit of willpower not to look at Renny.

We both feel like there's at least one more, he thought. But would it do any good to tell Seth that? I don't want to make these monks worry we're missing something. I don't want them to think they've failed somehow. Seth and Mino have been through a lot too. So shouldn't we keep this half-envisioned prophecy to ourselves? Maybe it's stopped for a reason. We weren't supposed to prophesy about it yet, for some reason... Fate's controlled so much of our lives. I'm making this decision now. And I think I'm right anyway.

"Well," he finally said to Seth, "if we ever have more visions, we'll tell you."

Renny nodded. "And I have a feeling we'll come back someday."

Seth remembered something and stood, came around the desk, and picked up an envelope from a pile on a chair. "Renny, if you could, give this to your brother. I can't get back State-side for a while, or I'd give it to him myself. Last time Lhamo spoke to him, your brother wanted to join the Kota community in Utah once he'd finished his PhD. I think he'd be graduated by now, correct?"

Renny nodded with a proud smile.

"If he's still interested, could you give this letter to him?"

Renny took the envelope. "Can I ask what it says?"

"It's Lhamo's thoughts on how your brother might help the people who come to us for assistance – counseling, that kind of thing. And I added in a personal note about how much his sister means to us." Seth winked.

Renny started to tear up again and went in for a hug. "I'll miss you."

"Miss you too, kiddo."

To Hazen's surprise, the big man reached out an arm and pulled him by the front of his robes to join their embrace.

"Oof." But Hazen laughed and hugged the old monk tight.

Seth released them, tears in his eyes. "I've grown very fond of you too, Hazen. What you four did here will mean a lot to the world someday. Maybe that time will be soon, maybe decades from now, maybe centuries. But these prophecies will matter. I really, truly believe that."

Hazen nodded his thanks and bowed low to the Kota monk.

Seth returned the bow, then smiled. "Okay, you two. Get out of here."

A few hours later, Hazen met Renny at the temple gates. He once again wore normal clothes, and the softness of his hoodie surprised him. Renny wore jeans, a sweater, and boots. She too looked as if she hardly remembered what real clothes felt like.

Together, they tossed their few bags into the back of the jeep they'd called from town. It'd take several hours to cross the beautiful terrain to Lhasa, where they had plane tickets waiting.

"Ready?" asked Hazen.

Renny opened the backseat door and climbed in. Hazen sat beside her, and when they were ready the driver started their long trek across Tibet. They sat in silence for some time, taking in the sights.

"So what do we do now?" Renny asked at last.

"I guess whatever we want. Weird feeling, right?"

She nodded. "Are you going to work for your dad at the World Space Program?" She scrunched her face. "When I had that dream about visiting your dad, I saw him offering you a job. That's part of what you two talked about when you left me in his library, right?"

He'd never suspected she knew this. "Yeah, Dad offered me a job. But I doubt it'd be a good fit." He looked down at his hoodie. "I'm not sure I'm cut out for a corporate environment."

She rolled her eyes with a grin. "I'm serious, Hazen. What do you want to do?" She looked out her window. "Now that our visions have stopped, there's no reason we *have* to stick together anymore."

He snorted. "Yes, there is. I'm in love with you."

Her head whipped around, eyes wide as she looked back at him. "Oh..."

Hazen leaned in and quickly kissed her on the lips. Then he sat back and grinned at her.

She smiled at him. "Well, in that case... How'd you feel about joining the Kota community in Utah with my brother? At least for a while, so we can show him the ropes. And I've kinda gotten used to doing good. Maybe we can help people there too. What do you think?"

"Sounds like a great idea."

9

The Interceder

Once in Lhasa, Hazen was starving and stopped at the market while Renny went ahead to the airport. He couldn't help but remember being here with the others. When they'd first arrived, they had to wait for their ride to Gyantse, so they'd killed time by touring the holy sites of Lhasa. Hazen had pointed out a modern fire extinguisher on the side of a half-ruined temple, and Oryan said, "That's a little too on the nose, don't you think?" This had made them all laugh, but it was also sobering as they explored the ancient city and its splashes of the West.

The Lhasa market looked like Hazen remembered too. The shops were tightly packed. Tourists strolled and shopped, pointing and talking in excited voices. Few English-speakers were here, and Hazen realized how much he'd adapted to the constant sound of unknown language. Wafts of cooked meat made his stomach growl.

Ooh, thought Hazen. I miss fresh meat.

At a food stand, he ordered by pointing to the menu without shame. When he had his tray of food in hand, he turned into the common area of the market's dining tables. Hazen found a seat at an empty table, and he shrugged off his backpack to place between his feet. Dressed like a tourist, he pulled his hood further down his shaved head to avoid hawkers. After a satisfying sniff of his food, he dug into his plate of steaming bean noodles, dumplings, and stuffed sausage of undefinable meaty origin. The table next to him was occupied by tourists chatting about whatever they'd found interesting in the museum or the market. Hazen kept to his food and tried to ease back into relative civilization.

As he took a bite, someone set a bowl across from him. Hazen looked up from under his hood and saw a westerner dressed in a dark coat. The man looked like any number of businessmen he'd seen. There was nothing particularly interesting about him. He smiled at Hazen, his gray eyes studying Hazen's face.

"Mind if I join you?" He sounded American.

Hazen motioned with his utensil that the man was free to sit.

The man sat and glanced at his bowl of porridge with an odd look. He faced Hazen and again smiled. "I'm Troy Kandoya. Sorry if I'm bothering you – you looked deep in thought. But I've been stuck on a bus with locals for an hour and it'd be nice to speak English again."

Hazen managed to return the man's smile. "No, it's fine. I'm Hazen Stephenson. Nice to meet you." He wiped sauce off his hand and shook Troy's. He scowled in thought. "Kandoya... I know that name."

Troy shrugged but had a slight grin. "So what brings you to these parts?" His eyes lifted to Hazen's shaved head under his hood. "Pilgrimage?"

"Not exactly."

Why do I know that name? thought Hazen. Kandoya... I *know* that name.

"I was with a group," he said carefully. "We were on a soul-searching journey, I guess you'd call it." He took a bite of food and hoped he wouldn't have to explain more.

"Hmm." Troy hadn't touched his food. "On your own now?"

"No, my partner...girlfriend went to the airport already. We're going home, first to L.A., then Milwaukee for a while."

"Wisconsin?" Troy grinned. He was the chatty sort. "I'm originally from the Midwest myself. Small world."

Hazen saw no point in responding and shoveled more noodles into his mouth.

"Was it just the two of you traveling together?"

Hazen stopped mid bite and shook his head. "No, we came with friends. One of them was killed."

Troy watched Hazen's next several bites. His voice changed, sounding more somber now. "I'm sorry about your friend. These are strange times we live in. The end times, some say. Though I'd say it's only *an* end time. Ages come and go. Dynasties rise and fall." He lifted his hands to indicate their surroundings. "At several points in our history, we've feared *the* end. I imagine that will continue to happen for many futures."

A noodle slipped off Hazen's lip back into his bowl. He sat back, appetite forgotten. "You're one of us, aren't you?"

If this guy's legit, he thought, he'll know what I mean.

Troy rested his elbows on the table and continued to speak in his new tone. "No, Hazen. I'm not a prophet. Not exactly."

"But you know about us? About the Kota? Are you here to make me change some future?"

Troy shook his head. "No. I'd never make you do anything. However ironic it is, I'm a strong believer in free will."

"Ironic? Ironic how?"

"I am he who will do the work, and he who will do the work alone."

Hazen's mouth hung open. "You... What?"

Troy lifted an eyebrow.

"How do you know those words?"

"I'm the Interceder, the Bearer brother you and Renny Nado envisioned. I'm here from the future." He grinned. "I never get tired of saying that."

"You're..." Hazen swallowed.

Oh, my God, he thought. He really is who he says. He knows the words Renny planned for the prophecy, and she never told anyone but me.

"If you're the Interceder, why didn't you intercede and save Oryan?"

Troy frowned. "I'm afraid I can't change fated futures any more than you can, Hazen. I'm sorry about Oryan. Believe me, I am. But I did save Renny."

A busser came to their table. The young, native woman wore an American band T-shirt with a worker's pin declaring her name to be 'Kokko.'

Hazen knew exactly what Renny might've said, and he let out a short laugh before covering his face in his hands.

"You finished?"

"Yeah, sorry." Hazen sat back so she could take his tray.

Kokko looked at Troy's untouched porridge. "You finished too?"

Troy smiled at the native and nodded. "Yes. Turns out I wasn't hungry."

Not caring one way or the other, Kokko took their trays to dispose of the contents.

Hazen studied the man across from him. "You exist in the lights... You don't eat, do you?"

"Nope. No need. And no point. I can't taste or smell anything. If it makes you feel better, I have a weirder life than yours."

Hazen had a million questions, but he started with, "You saved Renny?"

"Yes. Vin thought he saw what was fated to happen to her, but...well, he was deranged. *I* saw what needed to happen with Renny's fate. I don't want to confuse you, so please don't ask more. The important thing is, she's alive."

Hazen let out a lungful of air as he thought this over.

"Hazen Stephenson..." Troy peered into his face. "The great Kota prophet. In all my travels, I've never met anyone I've wanted to meet half as much as you."

Hazen snorted a laugh.

"No, I'm serious, young man." Troy chuckled at this and rubbed his chin in thought. "Actually, you're my elder. I'm not sure how to address you."

"I'm *your* elder? But you're..." Then he understood. "Are you even born yet?"

"No. But, the future in your visions isn't as distant as you think."

Hazen remembered. "The WSP spacecraft..."

"Indeed." Troy grinned.

"But so many other things seemed more futuristic. We saw hover cars, that space station, glowing money, futuristic weapons-"

"Well, okay, yes. *That* future is a long way out yet." Troy waved this off. "But the virus. The swirls opening. The Kota traveling through the portal. That all happens in your lifetime, Hazen. This destined series of events kicks off relatively soon. I suppose you could say it's already begun with you prophets."

This was an odd thing to hear, and Hazen took a moment while absentmindedly looking at the people around the market.

"What you've seen matters, Hazen. What Renny's written will give those in the future hope that the world can be restored. You've given *me* the only direction I'll have."

Hazen made a face. "But we left the prophecies so vague. If that's the only instruction you'll have, *would* it be better to write things out exactly like we saw them?"

Troy sighed and looked past Hazen in thought. Then he chuckled. "We'll never know. What's done is done. This is how things are meant to go, for whatever reason."

"But why does fate not want the prophecies to be clear?"

"Hazen, trust me that the prophecies are meant to be this way. It's human nature to rebel. The more specifically we're told what to do, the more we fight it. If the prophecies gave a detailed account of the future, maybe we'd realize how hard they'd be and not even try."

Hazen thought on this.

"Besides," said Troy, "what if you wrote down everything verbatim but were wrong about something you saw? Those in the future might go off your false facts and make a huge mistake. Who knows? I'm sorry I can't explain it very well. But I've seen what *will* happen with several of these prophecies. Trust me that you've done a good thing."

Hazen felt moisture rising to his eyes.

Troy looked truly sorry for all he'd suffered. "Hazen, what you've done will give the Marked saviors of Earth the only guidance they'll have. Maybe that's the whole point – you've given a promise that the world can be better."

Hazen let out a breath.

"I came here," said Troy, "to thank you. And to give you some encouragement. I know after everything you've seen you must feel very...small. But this was all more important than you can imagine." He smiled. "Well, you know something about seeing futures, so perhaps you can imagine."

Hazen made a face of agreement.

"Anyway." Troy tapped his fingers on the table. "I have a favor to ask you."

"You're the Interceder. You need *my* help?"

"Well, like I said, this future isn't far off. The Bearers are born in your lifetime, after all." He winked. "So, in this near-ish future, I need you to do something." He fished in his coat pocket and drew out a small book. He handed it to Hazen.

It was a moleskin journal, like one he used to write in as a kid. Hazen lifted the cover to flip its blank pages. "What's this for?"

"I need you to write down the prophecies, in English. Keep this journal with you. Someday, I need you to give it to my Bearer brother. That, Hazen, is a game-changer. My brother will... Well, giving him that book of prophecies will set us on the correct path."

Hazen looked at the journal again.

I memorized the prophecies when Renny recited them for Seth, he thought. *Yeah, I could write them all. Lord knows we've learned the importance of copies.*

He looked back at Troy. "Can't I just write them now and give this back to you? Then you could get it to your brother whenever he needs it."

"It's meant to be you who gives it to him." Troy smiled. "And, when you meet my brother, I'd appreciate if you didn't mention *this* meeting. All this circular, changing the past from the future stuff confuses the hell out of people."

Hazen had some idea what Troy meant, so he nodded. "Okay." He looked at the journal again.

Renny and I might want a copy of the prophecies for ourselves anyway, he thought. *It'd certainly be nice to have them recorded in English. The monks never need to know we've got this journal. I probably shouldn't tell them about Troy either, since we're not telling them about our Interceder visions.*

The weight of responsibility settled back on his shoulders. "Are you sure this is up to me?"

Troy nodded. "You're not done yet, Hazen."

"But the visions have dried up now that..." He swallowed as he saw the man's secretive grin. "Shit. Our visions *do* start up again, don't they? Am I going to have nightmares the rest of my life?" Hazen heard his voice shake. "Do I become like Vin?"

"No," Troy insisted. "No, Hazen. I promise you, Renny, and Jazzmon remain sane and good to the end of your days."

Hazen tried to believe this. "Do we go back to Gyantse?"

"That's entirely up to you."

He snorted a laugh. "Sure it is."

Troy raised his hands. "I don't see alternate paths like you prophets. I only see what will definitely happen. So, naturally I know what you decide about your place with the Kota. But it *is* your choice."

Hazen tried to think of any questions Renny would want answered. "Why didn't we have more visions about *you*? We didn't see enough to make the whole prophecy."

"Ah, well. I'm not supposed to know my whole job until a certain time. I suspect you're meant to keep what you've seen of me to yourselves until the rest of the visions arrive. *Then* you write the Interceder Prophecy, and by then it'll be time for me to know."

"So we don't have more visions until after you're born? When's that?"

Troy mimed zipping his lips.

Hazen huffed but looked at the journal in his hand. "Can you tell me when I give this to your brother?"

Troy rose from his seat with another secretive grin, straightening his coat. "Oh, you'll figure it out."

Hazen made a face up at him. "Come on! You're from the future. You're the only person who can really guide us, and now-"

Troy laughed. "*You* guide *me*, Hazen. See, I told you all this circular stuff is confusing."

Hazen rolled his eyes.

Troy smiled one last time, then bowed farewell before walking out of the marketplace.

Hazen huffed again.

Well, he thought. I would've at least liked to see the Interceder open a portal. Good lord...

He looked at the empty journal in his hands. After another moment's thought, he reached for his backpack, tucked the journal inside, and rose from his seat. With a final inhalation of wonderfully meaty aromas, he walked out of the marketplace. Time to meet Renny at the airport.

She's gonna be pissed she missed this guy, he thought.

Then Hazen remembered. He had a third cousin named Pax Kandoya.

10

The Bearer

Fifty years passed.

Hazen was back in Canada, where he believed his adventure began the day he met Renny. It had all started here, and he suspected much would happen here again.

Leaning on his cane, Hazen took a wobbly step from the chauffeured car that had brought him to this cemetery. The pavement was wet from earlier rain. He saw through his thick glasses that the few trees of the cemetery dripped rainwater from their budding leaves. Hazen used his cane to step off the road onto green grass. Before approaching the funeral gathering, he inspected his dark coat and monk robes underneath.

This combo probably looks weird, he thought. Oh, well, I never did dress properly for the occasion.

With a grin, he proceeded along the lane of tombstones. When he arrived at Pax Kandoya's burial site, Hazen leaned on his cane to inspect the mourners. He recognized a few distant relatives in the black-attired crowd. Pax had led a good life, and many tears were shed for their beloved cousin, uncle, friend, and father.

Hazen spotted the one man he was certain he recognized.

There's Troy, he thought. Wow, he barely ages a day...

The pastor at the head of the casket was saying, "Pax leaves behind many who love him. Sister Hipstra and brother-in-law Binx. Niece Marybeth. Nephews Elliot and Connor."

Hazen smiled at the next generation's normal names. Those his age had suffered from their parents' choices and gone the other way for their children.

I'll have to remember to tell Renny when I get home, he thought.

"Sons Troy and Lee," the pastor continued.

Hazen looked at the man beside Troy.

There he is, thought Hazen. The other Bearer brother. He's the one I must talk to and convince to join the Kota.

Over the years, as the number of Kota grew worldwide, those in Tibet decided it was best to establish a Kota Council of elders to help guide their followers. Naturally, as the two remaining original prophets, Hazen and Renny were asked to join this Council. Jazzmon had died in Scandinavia a few years before, or else Hazen knew she too would've been asked. As for Renny and himself, they secretly knew their work as prophets was not yet finished, so they'd accepted positions on the Council. And *this* was how they'd set in motion the fulfillment of their prophecies. Because of their fame and reputation, it was easy to convince the other Council members that the Kandoya brothers were the chosen Bearers they'd envisioned so long ago.

Hence Hazen's trip to Canada now.

He pulled out the aged journal from his coat. Now, the pages were no longer blank. Along with the prophecies he'd made with Renny, Jazzmon, and Oryan, he'd written several prophecies that had come to newer prophets over the years. Few were anything like the distant-future visions the original prophets had seen, but they were noteworthy in their own way. Many had already been fulfilled, and Hazen thought they added a sense of hope to the book.

Breaking up his thoughts, the funeral gathering dispersed. Hazen watched as Troy Kandoya reached into his pocket and pulled out a phone. The Interceder-to-be lifted a finger at his brother and walked off to answer the call.

Okay, thought Hazen, here we go.

He stepped with his cane over to Lee Kandoya, who was shaking hands and thanking people for coming. His wavy, brown hair blew in the breeze, but he didn't seem concerned about his appearance. His eyes looked as if he'd cried earlier, but now he was politely strong for his family and father's friends.

When Hazen's turn at the end of the line arrived, he shook the young man's hand. "So sorry for your loss. We never met, but I'm a third cousin of your father's."

"Oh." Lee's smile was warm and genuine. "How good of you to come, sir."

Hazen held up the book. "Do you have a moment? I wish to discuss something with you."

Lee glanced at the departing crowd, then gave Hazen his full attention. "Of course. What would you like to discuss?"

"The future." Hazen smiled.

Excerpt from
The Kota (The Kota Series Book 1)

Lee's expression was one of complete confusion as he looked up from within the cryogenic bed and saw Trok kneeling beside him. Reviving him had been a shockingly easy procedure, but the Kota scientists with Trok had prepared for this their whole lives.

Lee coughed and struggled to sit up in the steaming cryo bed.

"It's alright," said Trok. "You're okay. Just take it easy."

He was so excited and relieved to see Lee alive that he nearly grabbed him in a long-overdue embrace. Instead, he placed a hand on Lee's shoulder to steady him. Trok was tense for several reasons, but first off he wanted to make sure Lee was okay.

He's my long-lost little brother, thought Trok. Please, oh, please, just let him be okay!

As the doctors examined him, Lee looked beyond Trok at the dozen men and women gathered. Then he looked around the lab-cave. Trok knew Lee would see immediately that a good deal of time had passed – the state of the lab-cave showed centuries of disuse. Trok and the descendents of the Kota remnant had always kept a careful eye on the place, but some things couldn't fight age. Faint running lights hummed overhead, but the balcony around their lower level had rusted long ago and collapsed in places. Most of the ancient machinery was broken. Only the life support functions remained intact, though the system had been repaired many times by the Kota assigned to guard over Lee throughout the years.

Lee looked back at Trok and examined his face. Lee himself had physically aged maybe ten to fifteen years while sleeping. Now middle-aged, his forehead was wrinkled. His hair and beard were peppered gray. His body underneath the medical scrubs appeared only minimally atrophic, though very pale.

"You..." Lee cleared his throat to find his voice. "You were frozen too?"

Trok lifted an eyebrow. "Not exactly. Let the doctors check you over, and then we'll take you out of here. I'll explain everything once we're safely away."

"These are the Kota?"

"Yes."

"How long has it been?"

Trok hesitated, knowing this would be hard, but there was no real way to ease into it. "Five hundred years."

Lee's eyes widened, but he'd been prepared for this. He asked no more as the doctors finished examining him.

The doctor in charge stood, lowered his x-ray scanner, and turned to Trok. "Sir, he's as stable as we could've hoped. I think we're safe to move him. He's weak and groggy, but that'll wear off soon."

"Good." Relieved by this news, Trok focused on the next concern. He lowered his voice so as not to worry Lee. "I don't want to stay here any longer than necessary. I'm sure Dominion patrols check this place on a daily basis in hopes of intercepting us."

"Good thing we brought soldiers, then."

Yes, thought Trok bleakly. Kota soldiers, anyway. And we've only got five with us. They'd be no match for Dominion drone soldiers.

"I'd rather we didn't have to use them," he told the doctor. "We can't afford getting caught in a firefight." He looked down at his brother.

The doctor nodded and turned to help his partners with their patient. Lee seemed curious about why the Kota deferred to Trok, but he allowed himself to be lifted into a wheelchair. Once he was ready, the whole group hurried for the ancient building's exit.

Outside, the warm sunlight pouring down didn't bother Trok's eyes. He looked over the wilderness beyond the crumbling gates, searching for danger. Trok saw Lee take a deep breath of fresh air and close his eyes to feel the sunshine. This once again reminded Trok how disconnected he was from everything around him.

But now Lee's with me, thought Trok. I'm not as alone anymore. I just hope he can handle this.

"No patrol activity in the area, sir," called a Kota soldier from his position near a hover hummer.

Trok snapped into action and took over wheeling his brother toward this soldier's vehicle. "Let's be sure we're gone before they arrive."

"Yes, sir." The soldier whistled to his partners. "Load up!"

The Kota doctors and soldiers piled into the other vehicles as Trok helped Lee into the backseat of their hover hummer. Once Lee was secure, Trok closed his door and stepped around the vehicle to climb in the other side. He watched as the first hummer started off toward the road.

So far, so good.

Inside the hummer, Trok ordered their driver to go. They took off smoothly, and Trok relaxed enough to face his brother. He remembered the last time they'd been here – at the lab-cave, in a hover vehicle, with a Kota driver.

Things are so different now, he thought.

Lee took a drink from a thermos the doctors gave him. "I don't think I can wait until we get to wherever it is you're taking me." He was coming to life a bit. "What's happened?"

About the Author

Sunshine Somerville has a degree in English Literature and self-published her first book at the ripe old age of nine. She currently lives on the beachy side of Michigan with her husband, daughters, and rescued dogs.

The Kota Series is a Science Fantasy epic based on youthful obsessions with X-Men, Star Wars, The Chronicles of Narnia, Dark Angel, and A Wrinkle in Time.

The Alt-World Chronicles is an Urban Fantasy series inspired by weird recurring dreams, a brainstorming session in the shower, and one ridiculously hot summer lived in Kansas City.

A Fairly Fairy Tale is Sunshine's first Middle Grade Fantasy book. She got the idea from her family's crest, which portrays a dragon shooting flames from both ends, and from a niece whose second favorite word is farts.

www.SunshineSomerville.com

www.ingramcontent.com/pod-product-compliance
Lightning Source LLC
LaVergne TN
LVHW010454160826
845677LV00012B/2480

9798230338376